You're Next

The second DS Scarlett Macey novel.

Michael Fowler

Fiction aimed at the heart
and the head...

Published by Caffeine Nights Publishing 2017

Published in Great Britain by
Caffeine Nights Publishing
4 Eton Close
Walderslade
Chatham
Kent
ME5 9AT

www.caffeinenights.com

British Library Cataloguing in Publication Data.
A CIP catalogue record for this book is available from the British Library

ISBN: 978-1-910720-89-9

Also available as an eBook

Cover design by
Mark (Wills) Williams

Everything else by
Default, Luck and Accident

Following retirement, after thirty-two years as a police officer, working mainly as a detective, Michael returned to the deadly business of murder, as a writer. His past work brought him very close to some nasty characters, including psychopaths, and gruesome cases, and he draws on that experience to craft his novels: There is nothing gentle about Michael's stories.

His landmark novel *Heart of the Demon*, published in 2012, introduced Detective Sergeant Hunter Kerr. Michael has since written five novels and a novella featuring Kerr. He also released the first DS Scarlett Macey book in 2016. Michael is also the author of a standalone crime novella and a true crime thriller.

Michael has another side to his life – a passion for art, and has found considerable success as an artist, receiving numerous artistic accolades. Currently, his oil paintings can be found in the galleries of Spencer Coleman Fine Arts.

He is a member of the Crime Writers Association and International Thriller Writers.

Find out more at www.mjfowler.co.uk

Like Michael on Facebook

THE DS HUNTER KERR TITLES

HEART OF THE DEMON
COLD DEATH
SECRETS OF THE DEAD
COMING, READY OR NOT
SHADOW OF THE BEAST
BLACK & BLUE (e-book novella)
REAP WHAT YOU SOW (short story)

THE SCARLETT MACEY SERIES

SCREAM, YOU DIE

OTHER NOVELS

CHASING GHOSTS (short book)

NON-FICTION

SAFECRACKER (The true story of Britain's most infamous
safe blower)

To Liz, my best friend, my shoulder to lean on, my one and only.

YOU'RE NEXT

To my beautiful Granddaughter, Scarlett Macey Fowler.

One

In the Witness Room of Croydon Law Courts, Detective Sergeant Scarlett Macey was watching the clock above the door to Court One and taking slow, deep breaths, trying her best to calm her nerves; this wasn't unusual – she always felt like this at court, though today her anxiety level was up a few more points than usual. Today was the opening session of one of her biggest cases to date – the trial of serial rapist James Green: it had been four months since she had ended 'The Lycra Rapist's' reign of terror.

Earlier that morning, while going through her statement over breakfast, flashbacks of the case had visited Scarlett. In particular, snapshots of the self-righteous grin Green had tormented her with throughout his interview. She wondered if he was still so full of himself, having spent the first four months of this year behind bars?

Seeing James Green remanded to prison by the Magistrates had been one of her most gratifying moments as a detective. His incarceration had brought relief to the female population of Richmond in general and students in particular: last summer four young women had been sexually assaulted, and three others raped, by a knife wielding, Lycra-clad, maniac. Scarlett ended his campaign when she caught him in a sting operation – an undercover officer, posing as a student, had lured him into an attack.

Being caught in the act should have made things easy but the interview that followed had been frustrating – he'd denied everything, despite being identified, even having the audacity to state that he didn't attack the undercover officer, but 'merely pushed her away', because he believed she was a prostitute propositioning him for sex. Scarlett had taken an instant dislike to his conceited arrogance, and took great pleasure in facing him in the custody suite and charging him with three rapes and an attempted rape, the day after his arrest. She'd felt even greater satisfaction in childishly waving him off in the prisoner transport bus to High Down Prison, where he had since been detained.

Since then, because of other pressing matters within the department, his arrest had drifted into distant memory, but had resurrected itself over the past couple of days as Scarlett focused on preparing herself for the trial. In particular, it had invaded her thoughts last night, unsettling her sleep as she rehearsed a list of answers for the tough line of expected questions from the defence. In spite of feeling tired, she had arisen in buoyant mood.

Now though Scarlett wasn't feeling so upbeat. For the past ten minutes she'd been sitting at a table in the witness room, switching her gaze between the clock and the blank screen of her BlackBerry, trying her best to hide her concern. It was 10 a.m. and her main witness had not yet arrived.

She had rung Claudette Jackson yesterday afternoon to check she was okay – one of the many reassuring calls Scarlett had made during these past four months – and although Claudette's voice had sounded fragile she'd confirmed she was still prepared to give evidence against the man who had viciously raped her. Scarlett had ended the call by asking her to be at court for 09.30, so that they could go through her evidence one final time before the trial started. Claudette not being here was worrying; she was their last opportunity to prosecute serial rapist Green: since his remand, the Crown Prosecution Service had been forced to drop two of the rape charges because both of his victims had been deemed medically unfit to give evidence; one of the girls had been hospitalised after a nervous breakdown and then diagnosed with Post Traumatic Stress Disorder, while the other had been so disturbed since the attack that she had locked herself away in her bedroom and refused to speak to Scarlett: a month ago she had also been diagnosed with PTSD.

Over the past quarter of an hour Scarlett had called Claudette's mobile every couple of minutes but it had rung out and then diverted to voicemail. She had left messages for Claudette to ring her back, but the pleas had gone unanswered. The last time she had rung – two minutes earlier – Scarlett had tried to hide the tension in her voice.

'She's probably got stuck in traffic.'

DC Tarn Scarr's voice broke Scarlett's concentration. Dragging her gaze away from her BlackBerry, she eyed her working partner seated opposite. He was leaning back on his chair fiddling with his dark blue tie, tightening the knot into his white button-down collar. She gave a worried half smile, 'I hope so. I hope it's nothing else. She was nervous on the phone yesterday. I hope she's not had second thoughts.'

'You worry too much Scarlett. Claudette'll be here. She said so, didn't she?' He finished with his tie, flicked away invisible flecks from it.

Scarlett smiled to herself. Tarn had fussed over his appearance throughout the four years she'd known him. He was the best dressed guy in the office and checked himself every time he passed a mirror. All the Homicide Squad pulled his leg about it. Scarlett glanced down at the blank screen of her phone again, willing it to ring. 'I told her to be here for 9.30, that the court started at ten. It's gone ten o'clock now.'

'Only just. Give her another couple of minutes and then try her again.' Tarn pulled the front of his jacket together and scrutinised the alignment.

Scarlett was about to respond when the door to the courtroom opened and in walked the CPS barrister leading their case. Scarlett had first met Katherine Nicholson six weeks earlier at a pre-trial review of the evidence. Katherine was in her late forties, but her unblemished features made her look younger. She was in court attire, wig partly covering a shoulder length bob of shiny light brown hair. The first time Scarlett had set eyes upon her across the conference table she'd admired how elegant Katherine looked. If things hadn't turned out the way they had for her, maybe Scarlett could have been a barrister, enjoying the lifestyle trappings that came with it, instead of being a put-upon Detective Sergeant in an overstretched Homicide Squad.

A welcoming smile on her face, the barrister made a bee-line for her.

Scarlett stood.

'James Green is downstairs in the cells. Are we all good to go?' Katherine asked cheerily, rubbing her hands.

'We are,' Scarlett replied, pointing to herself and Tarn, 'but our main witness is not here yet.'

Katherine's smile disappeared and her face creased into a frown. 'Delayed?'

Scarlett shrugged, 'Don't know. I've tried ringing her mobile and she's not answering. I rang her yesterday afternoon and confirmed everything with her. I don't know where she is.'

The barrister pushed back the sleeve of her gown and glanced at her watch, 'Well they're just selecting the jury now. The trial's scheduled for starting at eleven – in fifty minutes' time. Does she live far away?'

'Twickenham.'

'Well look, can I suggest you get yourselves over to her place and see what's happening with her? I'll go and have a word with the judge and request a short adjournment. I'm sure he'll approve, he knows of the difficulties we've had with the other witnesses in this case.' She looked at her watch again. 'I'll ask for a twelve o'clock start. Meet me back here at quarter to twelve.' With a reassuring smile, she turned on her heels and made her way back to the courtroom door.

Scarlett scooped up her bag and phone, nodded at Tarn for them to go, and speed-dialled Claudette Jackson's number again as she made for the exit.

Two

They headed out of Croydon on the busy A23 towards Twickenham, where Claudette Jackson rented a two-bedroom semi with a friend from university.

Scarlett ended yet another call to Claudette's mobile – it had again diverted to voicemail. She stared out through the windscreen, gazing at an endless ribbon of traffic before them. They were moving, but not very fast. She would have loved to have switched on the blues and twos but she didn't have that option – they were in Tarn's car and not a squad car. Anxiety was again beginning to take hold – she could feel her chest tightening. She inhaled deeply, and breathing out slowly said, 'I'm getting a bit worried.'

Tarn kept his eyes on the road. 'There'll be some simple explanation. She said she was coming.'

As they entered Twickenham, Scarlett directed Tarn away from the main stretch of road into the estates. After negotiating a number of streets, they pulled up outside a 1960s red brick end town house. Part of the front garden had been block-paved and an aged blue Nissan Micra was parked on the drive.

'That's her car,' said Scarlett, opening the passenger door while pushing her mobile into her jacket pocket. Shutting the door with a swing of her hip, she studied the front of the house. The curtains were closed, upstairs and downstairs. She had a bad feeling about this. With Tarn following, Scarlett walked quickly to the front door and rapped hard. It was solid wood and stung her knuckles. She waited a few seconds, and when there was no answer, banged again, this time with the side of her fist.

Still no answer.

'Let's try the back,' she said over her shoulder, and walked around the side. The back door was also wooden, although the top half panels contained frosted glass. The kitchen window blinds were partly open. Scarlett cupped her hand against the glass and peered through the gaps. The kitchen was small – though slightly larger than her galley one back home. Nothing looked out of place. She turned back to the door and knocked. After a few seconds without a response she tried again. Nothing. Scarlett looked around to see if there was anywhere obvious that a key might be hidden. Two wheelie bins were parked close to the back fence and she shuffled them aside to check beneath but there was no secreted key. She said to Tarn, 'Let's see if any of the neighbours are in. Maybe they've seen her?'

After returning to the front of the house they tried the adjoining neighbour's home. Scarlett's knock was immediately answered by a shout of 'Just a minute,' followed by the sound of shuffling feet approaching. The front door opened a fraction on a chain and an elderly man's unshaven face appeared in the gap. He gave her the once-over, his eyes trailing up to her deep-red dyed hair, and his enquiring look turned to one of suspicion. Scarlett smiled to herself; it was the usual first response people gave her. It then generally turned to one of disbelief when she told them she was a cop. She greeted him with an engaging smile in an attempt to disarm his wariness, and then announced who she was, holding up her warrant card for him to see.

He scrutinised it carefully and glanced at her hair, before meeting her look. 'Police! Is there something up?'

Scarlett told him there was nothing wrong and that they just wanted to speak to his neighbour Claudette Jackson.

The man closed the door a second to unclip the chain and then opened it fully. He was dressed in a sweatshirt, baggy joggers and slippers and looked to be in his late sixties or early seventies. 'Do you know if she's in?' she enquired.

The man stepped onto the path and gazed at Claudette's house. 'Her car's there, but I haven't seen her this morning. It's not usually there at this time. She's usually gone to work in it by now. I heard her friend, Rachel, go early doors. They're teachers. Different schools though. They have told me where they work but I've forgotten. I think Rachel's at Archdeacon Cambridge.

That seems to ring a bell. She's good to me. Always asks me how I am – my health not being how it is…'

'You've not seen Claudette go out then?' Scarlett cut him short. She wasn't being rude, but she had concerns about Claudette and no time to listen to someone's health problems.

The man took a wobbly step along the path and looked up at the bedroom windows. He shook his head. 'No. Like I say she's usually up and gone by now. I don't normally hear the pair coming back until sixish, but it looks to me as though Claudette's still in bed. Her curtains are normally open at this time of day. Maybe she's not very well. Have you tried banging?'

Scarlett told him they had. Front and back doors.

He shrugged his shoulders.

'You haven't got a spare key, have you?'

'No.'

Scarlett thanked the man for his help and turned back to Tarn. 'Come on, we'll give it another knock. I'll try her mobile again.'

They returned to the front door. The neighbour remained on his path watching them over the fence. Scarlett gave him a smile and thumped Claudette's door again. After waiting for the best part of twenty seconds, with no response, she bent down, opened the letter box, speed-dialled Claudette's mobile and pressed an ear close to the open flap. After a few seconds, she heard a soft ringing tone. The tinny sound mimicked that of an old-fashioned phone and seemed to be drifting down from the first floor. She looked up at Tarn. 'Her phone's ringing. I can hear it. Something's not right. We need to get in there. Now!'

Three

At 5' 8" Tarn wasn't very tall but he was solid, and it only took him two flying kicks to send the back door crashing in, whereupon they dashed into the kitchen and up the stairs. The neighbour had said Claudette's bedroom was at the front, so they doubled back at the top of the stairs and Scarlett anxiously pushed open the facing door. The room was in gloom, the only light coming from a gap in the curtains, but it was enough for them to pick out Claudette's body, draped over the edge of her three-quarter bed. Below her head, on the carpet, was a crusting pool of vomit. Her eyes were shut, and her mouth open and some of the sick had dried around her lips. Scarlett didn't need to check her to know she was dead. She did a quick scan of the upper body, looking for signs of violence. There was none visible, and her gaze diverted to the bedside table where she saw a wine bottle, a wine glass, with what appeared to be the last dregs of some white wine in the bottom, and next to that an upturned small brown tablet bottle and a couple of small white pills near the open top. She also spotted a handwritten note next to Claudette's mobile.

'Shit!'

Tarn switched on the light and the room was instantly bathed in warm radiance. It caught Scarlett by surprise and made her jump. She glanced at the letter. It was on an A5 sheet of lined paper with a serrated edge where it had been torn from a pad. Scarlett wasn't carrying any protective gloves – she had dressed for court, and not work that morning – so she edged closer to the note and scanned it, leaning over without touching it. The message read:

It is now 19 weeks since I was raped and no matter how much I have tried to put it behind me I feel as though I will never be the person I was before it happened. I relive the event every night. It won't go away and there is only one way out I can see to stop all my pain. I'm so sorry for the distress for whoever finds me. If it's you Rachel I am really sorry – you are the bestest friend I ever had. Thank you for all the hours you have spent listening to me and trying to help. There were times when I felt stronger because of your help, but then the nightmares took me back to square one. Also sorry to my mum. I love you mum. You might not understand but I will be at peace, believe me. Say a pray for me. Tell Detective Macey that I'm sorry as well. Tell her I appreciate everything she's done for me. I thought I could face my attacker, but I realise I can't and never will be able to. I just pray James Green gets what's coming to him even though I won't be around to see it.

Once again, I'm sorry.

Claudette x

'Aw Fuck! ' Scarlett looked down at Claudette. Only her upper body was on display – a duvet covered her lower half. She couldn't help but notice how painfully thin Claudette was – her ribs were visible and her tawny skin no longer had the lustre she enviously remembered from their first meeting.

Following Green's arrest, Scarlett had appealed for victims to come forward and Claudette left a message on the incident room number that she wanted to speak to a detective about James Green. Scarlett had called her back and they had arranged to meet somewhere quiet, where Claudette might feel comfortable about opening up. Scarlett and Tarn met her the next day, in a café overlooking the river, and over coffee, after spending some considerable time putting her at ease, they managed to tease out of her details of how she had been raped at knifepoint and now lived in constant fear that she would be killed.

She had brought them here, to the home she shared with her friend, and handed over the clothing she had been wearing during that attack – hidden in a bin-liner beneath her bed. That evidence had been crucial – it had given them his DNA. That had been the easy part. The hard part had been back in the Victim Interview Suite, getting Claudette to repeat everything she had told them and for her to be medically examined by a police doctor. It was a painful experience for Claudette, but Scarlett had recognised the signs; experience told her that Claudette needed regular contact and Scarlett had kept in touch, but at no time during their half a dozen meetings did she get the feeling Claudette was suicidal. In fact, she'd thought Claudette was growing stronger despite her unease about attending court. As Scarlett looked down at the skinny, lifeless body, she felt pangs of guilt and wondered if her phone call yesterday afternoon had been the trigger for this. She wondered how long Claudette had been dead. Turning to Tarn, she said, 'Fuck, fuck and fucking fuck!'

'Christ, Scarlett, I never thought she'd do this.'

'Me neither. Me-fucking-neither.' Giving Claudette's corpse one more glance, Scarlett took in a steadying breath and concentrated on her partner. 'Right we need to call this in. Request the on-call FME and get SOCO here.' She glanced at her watch. 'I'll need you to take charge of this scene. I'm going to have to shoot back to court, speak to the barrister and tell her what's happened. See if we can get an adjournment.' She held out a hand, 'I'm going to need your car.'

Tarn threw her an astonished look.

Her partner drove a 3-year-old BMW, which was as always immaculate, and his pride and joy but right now she had no other option. She held out her hand again. 'Come on, don't give me that look, I'll treat it as if it was my own.'

'You don't have a car. You ride a motorbike.'

'So, I'll be more careful then won't I? Promise. Now give me your keys. This is not up for debate – I need to get back to court and pronto.'

Four

Scarlett drove back to court with her head in turmoil. An hour and a half ago she was all prepared to go head-to-head with James Green's defence counsel, determined to make sure that Green was hung out to dry for his crimes. Suddenly everything was in the balance. *What a crock of shit.*

She made it back to court five minutes before the agreed time, and after hurrying through security sought out Katherine Nicholson. The CPS barrister imbued an air of calm, whereas Scarlett was hot and flustered and still breathing heavily from her dash.

Swallowing hard, Scarlett explained what they'd found.

'And you think its suicide?'

'She left a note which indicates she intended to take her own life and we've found pills next to her body. We don't know what they are yet, but they look like prescription tablets.'

'Oh my. I am sorry.' The barrister's face was grim. 'This is not good news. I don't just mean about Miss Jackson, but about the trial.'

Scarlett frowned. 'It's bloody awful about Claudette, but we can still use her evidence. New rules permit it, don't they?'

'They do DS Macey, but in this case I fear her evidence will be not much use.'

'Not much use?' Scarlett could feel herself getting uneasy.

'When I requested the short adjournment with the judge, the defence barrister had to be there, and Mr Skelton QC disclosed Green's defence is that he had sex with Claudette Jackson in the grounds of Richmond University but it was consensual.'

Katherine Nicholson's reply brought her up quick. It wasn't just her words, it was hearing the name of the defence barrister representing James Green. She couldn't stop herself blurting out, 'Thomas Skelton?'

'Yes. Do you know him?'

Do I know him! Do I fucking know him! Taking a sharp breath, maintaining her composure, she replied, 'I've come across him.' That was a lie. She had done more than come across him. Twelve years earlier they'd been lovers. Tom was a year above her when she was studying Law at University and she had instantly fallen for his good looks and charm. She had lost her virginity to Tom and been madly in love with him. She was sleeping with him the night the police told her that her parents had been killed; the night when her entire life changed. She tumbled his name around inside her head. Thomas Skelton QC; her once best friend, her one-time lover, the man she thought she was going to marry and be happy ever after with, was defending scumbag, low-life, serial rapist, James Green. How could he do this to her? *The treacherous bastard!*

Taking another quick breath and bringing back her thoughts to what Katherine Nicholson had said, she spat out, 'Consensual! He held a knife to her throat. He threatened to kill her.'

'We know that, but the jury doesn't. Green is going to deny it. His defence are going to say that he chatted up Miss Jackson at the bar where she worked and asked her out. We know from Miss Jackson's testimony some of that is right.'

'Yes, it is. Green did chat with her on a couple of occasions, and bought her drinks, but when she realised he was hitting on her she ignored him. In fact, she told some friends and pretended to flirt with one of the guys to put him off. It's my belief he targeted her because of that. Revenge!'

'You and I both believe that, but it can't be brought in as evidence. We can only introduce fact. And the facts, which Green's defence will introduce, are not too far away from Miss Jackson's testimony. The only difference being she states she was raped at knifepoint and he says the sex was consensual. It's her word against his and we have no other witnesses.'

'Then why didn't he say that when I interviewed him following his arrest?'

'I've raised that point, and his defence says Green told him that the moment he pushed the undercover detective you had it in for him. That you'd made up your mind he was guilty.'

Scarlett let out an exasperated snort. 'Rubbish! You've seen our interview. Pushed the detective away! DC Ella Bloom was posing as a student in Richmond University grounds and he attacked her. If we hadn't been close by to arrest him she would have been his next victim.'

'I'm sure that's the case, but Green stated DC Bloom propositioned him for sex, and he thought she was a prostitute, which is why he pushed her away. We already decided to not proceed with that charge in light of the evidence.'

'DC Bloom told it as it happened. She was telling the truth.'

'I'm sure she was, but we know from recent trials that evidence from undercover officers is fraught with danger unless backed up with some evidence to support it, ie, taped evidence.'

'We couldn't get clearance for DC Bloom to wear a wire.'

'I know how difficult this is for you DS Macey. You know yourself how difficult rape trials are to prosecute, even where we do get witnesses to go into the box to give evidence. Given what's just happened to Miss Jackson we aren't in a position to challenge what Green will be saying in his defence.'

'You're telling me that we're not going to go to trial,' said Scarlett.

'I'm saying that in light of what's happened to our witness there is very little prospect of us getting a conviction.'

'So Green is going to be allowed to go, even though he's raped three women. And they're just the ones we know of!'

The barrister looked sad. 'I will be having a word with the judge, DS Macey, but I already know what his response is going to be once I present this latest information.'

'There's nothing you, or we, can do to change this?'

'I'm genuinely sorry DS Macey, but I firmly believe that now we can no longer corroborate the evidence we have it will not be enough to convict James Green.'

'So we let a serial rapist walk free?' Scarlett didn't wait for the CPS Barrister to answer. Clenching her fists and biting back an oath, she turned and quick-stepped to the exit, doing her best to remain professional despite the fury eating away inside.

Five

Outside the advocates' robing room Scarlett waited, trying to control her temper. She had been there half an hour. She'd changed her mind about leaving and doubled back into court. Scarlett wanted her moment. The charges against James Green had been formally dropped and the trial judge had released him. Green was downstairs in the cell area awaiting transport back to prison to collect his things before he was freed.

Free to go on the rampage again, she seethed to herself as she leant against the wall.

Scarlett had just taken out her mobile to check the time – conscious that she had left Tarn alone to deal with Claudette's death – when the door to the robing room opened. Thomas Skelton appeared in the doorway, dressed in an expensive looking charcoal grey pinstripe suit, carrying a briefcase. It had been a good ten years since she had last seen her former lover but she recognised him immediately, even though his once collar length brown hair was now shorter and thinner on top and he had put on some weight, especially around the middle. The change in him was not for the better and the spark to a flame emotion he had so frequently ignited in her back then was no longer there. By the reaction on his face, he recognised her.

'Scarlett!' he said.

She sprang forward, slipping her phone back into her jacket pocket. 'How could you, Tom?'

'How could I what?'

'Green.'

He sighed, 'I didn't know you were the officer in the case until I'd taken the job.'

His voice was plummy. That was new and it sounded nauseating. She returned, 'You could have refused it.'

'His solicitor is a personal friend. He wanted me to take it.'

'He raped three women. Possibly more!'

'Allegedly raped three women!'

'Bullshit!' She took a deep breath. 'I thought you were different.'

'Different?'

'Different to all the other defence shysters. I thought you had morals'

'You've got your job to do Scarlett and I've got mine. You're making this too personal.'

'Personal! Personal! 'Course it's fucking personal. He's a rapist, for Christ's sake.'

'Why don't you let me buy you a coffee and we put this behind us.' He added, 'You look great by the way. Love the hair, suits you. Scarlett by name and Scarlett by hair.' He laughed at his own joke.

Scarlett took a couple of imperceptible breaths to calm herself down. The anger inside was close to boiling point. He was treating the issue like a mere misdemeanour; she wanted to whack him one for what he had just said. 'You have got to be joking. I don't mix with the enemy.' Through gritted teeth she added, 'Do you know Tom, I thought I could trust you.' She jabbed a finger, 'But you know what? You're an arsehole just like all the other defence lawyers!' She was about to turn and leave but before parting she couldn't resist one final dig, 'Oh and by the way you don't look great. You're fat and bald.' Before he could respond Scarlett shot him a fiery glare, turned on her heels and stormed off.

Six

By the time Scarlett returned to Claudette's house, two funeral attendants were wheeling her out of the front door in a body bag on a gurney. She watched them place the body into the back of the blacked-out undertaker's van and then drive slowly away. Most of the neighbours were out, their faces solemn.

Scarlett fob-locked Tarn's car, and with heavy heart stepped around Claudette's parked Nissan Micra and went in through the open front door. Tarn was just coming down the stairs carrying an armful of exhibit bags.

He shot her a surprised look. 'I didn't expect to be seeing you so quick. Has it been adjourned for the day?'

'There's not going to be a trial. CPS has bottled it. No chance of a conviction they say.' She knew part of what she said wasn't true, but it was how she wanted to express her anger at the decision not to prosecute James Green.

Tarn stopped halfway down the stairs. 'So, what's happening to Green?'

'They've released him.'

'Released him?'

Scarlett threw up her hands, 'He's getting off Scot free! Raped three fucking women and we can't present any of the evidence!'

'I can't believe it!'

'You can't believe it.' Scarlett shook her head. 'I feel like fucking shit. That's just not justice.' She let off a weighty sigh, 'But right now there's nothing we can do about that. Anyway, bring me up to speed with this job. I've just seen them taking Claudette's body away.'

'The FME's been. She says there's no sign of violence on Claudette. The tablets she's taken are Amitriptylin. They're for depression, but they also help you sleep.' He held up one of the see-through plastic evidence bags to reveal a small brown medicine bottle. 'The name of the pharmacy is on the label so I'm going to get her GP's name and confirm she was prescribed them.' He continued his way downstairs. 'And you've only just missed SOCO. They've examined the scene and taken quite a few photos. It doesn't look suspicious. The PM is fixed up for tomorrow, that will confirm if it was an overdose.'

'What about contacting her family? Didn't the note mention her mother?'

Tarn nodded. 'Yeah I've recovered her mobile and scrolled through it. I've got a number for her mum, and I've got Rachel's number, the girl she shares this house with. I've found some paperwork. Her friend's full name is Rachel Crompton, and the neighbour was right, she does work at Archdeacon Cambridge's. Are we going to break the news to her?'

'We'll need to. From speaking with Claudette, I know they were really good friends. They met at uni and shared student accommodation. When Rachel finished her degree and got her teaching post she found this place and Claudette decided to rent with her. Rachel's been supporting her since the rape.'

Tarn nodded, 'Okay, I'm going to contact her first and break the news and then see if she has an address for Claudette's mother. I'd rather give her mum the bad news in person than a phone call.'

'I'd rather we do both personally. Especially because of how good friends she was with Rachel. Come on, we'll secure the back door as best we can and then drive over to the school where she works.' Scarlett sighed. 'I'm certainly going to need a drink by the end of today. I've not had a day as bad as this in a long while.'

Seven

Archdeacon Cambridge's Roman Catholic school was just off The Green at Twickenham. Finding it was easy, parking wasn't. Tarn left his car in the yellow no parking zone outside school and hoped no warden found it before they had finished their visit. At reception, Scarlett showed her identification and enquired after Rachel Crompton. The female receptionist told her she needed to speak with the Head and picked up the phone. Scarlett heard her say: 'Two detectives are here. They want to speak with Miss Crompton,' before hanging up. The young receptionist told them Mrs Harris would be along to see them shortly. No sooner had she finished speaking, when Scarlett heard the clip of heeled shoes behind her and turned to see a slim woman in her early forties making her way towards them. Mrs Harris had shoulder length blonde highlighted curly hair and wore a blue shift dress emblazoned with white and orange orchids. Although not her style, Scarlett admired the dress. They shook hands.

'You want to speak with Miss Crompton I understand?'

Scarlett nodded.

'It's nothing serious I hope? Nothing I should be concerned about?'

'It's about a good friend of hers. Claudette Jackson. The girl she rents with. We found her dead this morning and we need to have a chat with Rachel.'

'Oh goodness. I know Claudette. She came here a couple of months ago, asking if she could do her teacher training with us, but we already had a couple in. I'm really sorry to hear that. I know Claudette and Rachel are really good friends.' Pausing she said, 'Do you mind me asking, was it an accident, or something more serious?'

Scarlett shook her head, 'It looks like she took her own life. We just want to ask Rachel a few questions about how Claudette was when she last saw her.'

'Oh, that's terrible news! Of course I'll send for Rachel. She works in our reception class. We can wait in my study. It would be a better to talk to her in there. More private.'

The head asked the receptionist to go and fetch Rachel, and then led Scarlett and Tarn back down the corridor to her office.

Mrs Harris's room was a good size and bright. A bank of windows at the far wall let in strong afternoon sunshine. Her large desk was overflowing with paperwork, an open laptop sat in the middle of it. Cupboards crammed with books ran along the right-hand wall. There were three comfortable chairs in front of her desk and she offered them to Scarlett and Tarn and took up her own seat.

'Can I offer you a drink? Tea? Coffee?'

Scarlett declined, 'We only want to have a quick chat with Rachel. We shouldn't keep her too long.' She was about to ask how long Rachel had worked at the school when there was a soft tap at the door. Scarlett turned as a petite, dark haired girl, dressed in a loose-fitting blue tunic and matching blue trousers, entered the room. Her hair was tied back in a ponytail, exposing a heavily freckled face.

'This is Rachel,' announced the head.

Scarlett knew from her chats with Claudette that Rachel was a couple of years older than Claudette – but this girl looked a lot younger. She could imagine her being regularly asked for ID when she visited a bar.

The head said, 'Rachel these people are detectives, they want to speak with you about Claudette.'

'Claudette?' Her face creased into a puzzled frown.

Scarlett stood up and pointed to the spare seat, 'Hi Rachel, I'm Detective Sergeant Macey. Would you like to sit down?'

Rachel said, 'You're Scarlett.'

'Yes I am.'

'Claudette's talked about you. You're dealing with her case. Is that what this is about?'

'Yes I have been dealing with her case, but this is not what it's about.'

Rachel's face screwed up even more. 'What is it?'

'Rachel, please take a seat. I'm afraid I've got some bad news.'

Rachel's face paled. She grabbed hold of the chair back. 'I know what you're going to tell me. Claudette's dead, isn't she? I can tell by your face.'

Scarlett nodded. 'We found her this morning.'

'Where?'

'At your house. We had to break in. We found her in bed.'

Her hand shot to her mouth and she slumped into the chair. 'Oh my God, no!'

'I'm sorry to break this news to you Rachel.'

'How?'

'It looks like an overdose. We've found a few pills prescribed to her and an almost empty pill bottle on the bedside cabinet.'

'The ones she got from the doctors – to help her sleep?'

Scarlett nodded.

'I can't believe it. I know how badly she's been affected by all this but I thought she'd turned the corner. She seemed fine last night. We even talked about the case.'

'I know this has come as a shock, but I need to ask you some questions. Are you okay with that?'

Rachel gave a brief nod. 'I can't believe it.'

'The fact that you know about what happened to her makes my questioning easier. She told me that you've been supporting her and I know from speaking with her regularly that she valued that support.'

'I could see when it was getting her down and so I'd sit down with her and we'd talk things through.'

'That was helpful, believe me. How did she seem last night? You said she appeared fine.'

'To be honest I was surprised she was like she was. I thought she'd be feeling worried, or down, but she was quite chatty. I asked her how she was feeling about today – about giving evidence. I said I could take the day off to support her if she wanted me to but she said no, she had you to support her. But she did say she would be glad when it was all over. I asked if she was absolutely sure that she didn't need me there and she said yes, and that I wasn't to worry. We cracked open a bottle of wine and ordered a pizza from the takeaway. Last night was the best

I've seen her in a long time. We had a laugh about some of the things we'd got up to at Uni. She seemed totally relaxed by the end of the night. In fact, she opened another bottle and asked me to share it with her. I had a glass from it, but I knew I had to be up for work early, and so I told I didn't want any more and that I was going to call it a night. She said she'd finish the glass she was drinking and then call it a night herself. I'd been in bed about ten minutes when I heard her switching the lights off downstairs and going to the bathroom. Then I must have dropped off.'

'So she seemed well?'

'Absolutely. You say you think she might have taken an overdose. Are you sure? It couldn't have been an accident? You know with the drink – she took too many tablets by mistake?'

Scarlett shook her head. 'She left a note. It wasn't an accident.'

'Oh my God, I can't believe it. Poor Claudette. I should have been there for her.'

'There was nothing you could have done, Rachel. Nothing at all. She'd made her decision.' Scarlett's words drifted away and for a few seconds the room fell into silence.

Rachel broke the quiet, 'Have you told her mum?'

'She's next on our list.'

Eight

It was gone seven o'clock by the time they got back to the office, and the place was deserted. Scarlett made them a hot drink, and while Tarn booked in the exhibits, she typed up her preliminary sudden death report for the Detective Inspector, and attached it into an email for him, copying in the Detective Chief Inspector: she didn't trust DI Hayden Taylor-Butler – she had issues with him – the DCI was her support mechanism to prove it had been sent. She'd tried to ring the DI that afternoon, to fill him in as they had driven over to the school to speak to Rachel Crompton, but he hadn't picked up and so she had left him a message on his voicemail. He still hadn't got back to her and she guessed he was playing his games with her as usual rather than being too busy.

The death warnings, as they were called in police speak, had taken longer than anticipated. They had taken a statement from Rachel and then driven over to Claudette's mother's. She had taken the news badly. Not only broken down in fits of screaming, but got angry with them too – blaming them for her daughter's death. 'If you hadn't put pressure on her to give evidence, my Claudette would still be alive,' she'd screamed at them. They had been unable to console her, or calm her down, and when Scarlett had tried to leave a card with her details, with a promise to call her tomorrow, she'd thrown it back at her. They had tactfully taken their leave and driven back to the station, barely a word passing between them.

Scarlett printed off a copy of the memo and the death report and re-read them. She was impressed with the measure of detail she had put into her three-page report, especially given her sombre mood. Although she knew she didn't directly cause

Claudette Jackson to kill herself, she felt some responsibility, given that she had persuaded Claudette to give evidence at James Green's trial. Within her report she had been careful to include every visit and every telephone call to Claudette. It wasn't just to cover herself; she knew that tomorrow morning, when they sat around the table to review what happened today, all DI Taylor-Butler would be concerned about was what impact the collapse of James Green's trial would have on *his* department, and not what effect Claudette's death meant for her family and close friends.

He's such a wanker.

Placing the printed copies into her top tray, she turned to Tarn. The bundle of exhibits he had been booking in were piled up on his desk. It looked like he was close to finishing the logging of all the material evidence. She asked, 'Nearly done?'

He held up a brown paper bag. 'Just the last of the clothing she was wearing and that's me done.'

She closed down her computer. 'Fancy a beer?'

'I'd like to say yes, but I've got something on. I've got to get home.'

'Tarn Scarr refusing a beer?'

He surprised her with a sheepish look and she was about to comment but he turned his head away and she decided to hold her thoughts. Loudly clearing her throat she said, 'No problem, it's been a long day anyway. It may be wise avoiding a drink when you've just had the shitty day we've had.' Picking up her bag and dragging her jacket off the back of her chair she added, 'I'll see you in the morning.'

Nine

Sitting alone at a table by one of the large bay windows in the Pitcher & Piano, overlooking the Thames, Scarlett was slowly getting drunk. Evening was fading and the riverside lights at the edge of the towpath had come on, casting a series of shimmers across the pewter coloured water fast-flowing towards nearby Richmond Bridge. Her eyes rested on the two coxless crews dragging a couple of quadruple sculls out of the water. She couldn't help but notice how toned the mixed crews looked, and the men's muscular thighs captured her attention. She watched them pick up the two boats with ease and carry them across the towpath until they disappeared from view. Rowing was always something she'd fancied having a go at but had never got around to trying. It would have to wait for another time, she told herself. Just now, with the long hours she kept she had all on maintaining her running, never mind taking on anything else.

She looked down at the almost empty glass on the table. Despite the numbing feeling the wine had given her she still hadn't managed to shake off the anger, sadness and frustration eating away at her. She hated James Green. She especially hated Thomas Skelton – the man she had once loved. They had shared so much together at university. She'd been with Tom on Valentine's night in 2002 when the police broke the news her parents had been murdered. He had consoled and supported her all through the police investigation into finding their killer, repeatedly assuring her he would always be there for her – and he had never given her cause to doubt those words. Sadly, they had split up. Mostly it had been her fault. She was too wrapped up in her sorrow, and had slowly pushed him away on the pretence of throwing herself into her law studies – telling him it was what her parents would have wished. They had split up tearfully over a meal, wishing one another the best for the future and Tom had gone on to get his law degree and a placement with a very good law firm in London. She had gained a 2:1, but the need to discover who had killed her parents had driven her to join the Metropolitan Police instead of choosing law. Her younger sister Rose had been a suspect and Scarlett had spent the past ten years trying to find Rose and prove her innocence.

As the thoughts and images tumbled around in Scarlett's head she couldn't believe Tom had let her down after all he had promised. Betrayed her! Worse still, *he* had been responsible for releasing a serial rapist back out onto the streets. *Bastard!* Right now, all she wanted to do was quit her job, but that wouldn't resolve her issues with Green. He couldn't be allowed to get away with this. He had ruined lives and deserved to rot in prison. She wanted vengeance – and the only she could gain that was by staying a detective. She would start planning his downfall tomorrow.

Scarlett picked up her wine glass, downed the remains of her Pinot Grigio and then re-filled it with the last in the bottle. She caught the attention of one of the bar staff and pointing at the empty bottle, ordered another.

Ten

Scarlett awoke to the sound of Amy Winehouse singing *Rehab*. She slowly opened her eyes and looked around the bedroom, before gazing down at herself. She was wearing just her shirt, bra, and knickers and was lying on top of the duvet. She was confused. How had she got here? She couldn't even remember getting home. And who had switched the radio on downstairs? The sudden metallic crash of the lid shutting on her kitchen waste bin made her jump. Seconds later, the soft shuffle of footsteps sounded in the hallway. Whoever was there was starting to climb the stairs.

'Hello' she called out and then felt foolish. What a stupid thing to say if it was a burglar and yet her mind was telling her it couldn't be. A burglar wouldn't have switched on the radio.

Seconds later the bedroom door opened and her ex-boyfriend Alex King stepped into the room. His appearance caught her off guard and caused her even greater confusion, especially as it looked as though he had spent the night; wearing a creased grey T–shirt, he was unshaven, and his short dark brown hair was messy. He was carrying a steaming hot drink in one hand and a plate of toast in the other. In spite of a throbbing head and feeling sick, a buzz of excitement coursed through her.

He set down the cup and plate on her bedside table, went to the window and pulled back a curtain. A stream of bright sunshine lit the bedroom. 'Come on lazy bones, it's a lovely day outside.'

The sunlight hurt Scarlett's eyes and she covered them with her hand to block out the glare. 'There's no need for sarcasm,' she replied. Then conscious of her semi-undressed state, she grabbed the duvet and tugged it up over her bare legs and midriff. 'What are you doing here? Come to think of it, how did you get in?'

'You don't remember do you?'

As Scarlett searched her memory banks to re-run the previous evening's events she watched Alex's face break into his trademark mischievous sexy smile – the one that had captured her attention two years earlier and still had an amazing affect on her. Some days – like today – she could kick herself for making that decision to split from him. She still fancied him like mad. Their coming together – in the words of her dear departed dad – had been fate; they'd first met in the pub where she had drunk last night – Alex had been standing at the bar with some mates, she was celebrating her 29th birthday with friends. He had turned the moment she entered the room and fixed her with a look that made it obvious he was interested. She'd dismissed it with a glance and a pleasant smile but then her friends had commented that he was staring at her and every time she turned around his startlingly blue eyes and wicked smile targeted her. For a good two hours, she had played coy but that had ended after she'd got up from the table to go to the toilet. She'd only gone a few steps when the cocktails kicked in and in her light-headed drunkenness she had stumbled against him, spilling some of his beer. She'd tried to apologise but unusually found a lump emerging in her throat and it had taken her seconds to finally get out that she was sorry.

'No harm done,' he'd said, and locked eyes with her. 'I'm Alex by the way.'

His voice had been so husky and his name had danced around inside her head like a playful elf. After what had seemed like an eternity Scarlett finally told him her name and added with a slur, 'It's my birthday.'

'Well very happy birthday Scarlett. I hope you're having a good night.'

She didn't know why she'd said it, because it had been so cheesy, but after slowly casting her gaze over his tanned face – she later learned he had just returned from a fortnight in Ibiza – and well-toned physique, she had replied, 'I am now,' and then burst out laughing.

Alex and his mates joined in the laughter and she invited them to join her party. For the remainder of the evening she and Alex had talked and as time came for them to leave Alex had asked her if he could give her a birthday kiss. She had been unable to resist. The kiss had been one of the most lingering and intensely intimate she had ever experienced; she melted in his arms, said her goodbyes to her friends and left the pub with him almost in a daydream. They had gone on to an Italian restaurant and then taken a cab back to his place where they had ended up in bed. It had been a perfect evening and the start of their year-long, mostly physical, relationship which had ended ten months ago. They hadn't rowed or fought, quite simply, Scarlett had reacted how she had done with Tom – deliberately putting some space between them – telling Alex she thought things were going a little too fast and she wanted to cool it but remain friends. Alex had a pretty busy career that regularly took him away, and so he agreed, suggesting they keep in touch. Since then they had been in and out of each other's lives but he had a remarkable habit of turning up just when she needed cheering up and this morning was one of those occasions. She suddenly realised how much she had missed him wrapping his arms around her, especially in bed. With an apologetic smile, she said. 'I guess you're going to tell me how much I embarrassed myself, aren't you?'

'You didn't embarrass yourself but you'd had a few too many.'

His words brought her thoughts back. 'I had a shit of a day. The drink must have gone to my head, I hadn't eaten since breakfast.'

He gave her a scolding look. 'That's as may be, but you shouldn't drown your sorrows in drink. And certainly not alone.'

'How did you know where I was?'

'One of the lads who works behind the bar knows me from the gym. He recognised you and gave me a call.'

'Thanks Alex.'

'Scarlett you've got to stop taking things to heart. We all have shit days but we don't deal with them by getting drunk.'

'Okay, okay, I know. Lesson learned.' She massaged her aching head by way of reinforcing the comment.

He smiled again. 'Okay, lecture over. Now drink your coffee and take these.' He fished in his tracksuit bottoms and pulled out two tablets which he put beside her mug. He said 'Paracetamols. I somehow think you might need them.'

'You're having a go at me again.'

'Someone's got to,' he muttered.

She delivered another repentant look. 'Thank you. I'm very grateful. And thank you for rescuing me last night.' As Alex turned to leave she said, 'I need to ring Tarn to sort out my lift. Will you get me my BlackBerry from my bag?'

'I've already rung him and told him he doesn't need to bother – that I was dropping you off.'

'You've told Tarn I got drunk?'

'No, of course not. I told him we went out for some food last night and I crashed down on your sofa. Half of that is the truth.'

'Thank you, Alex. I owe you.'

'Big time.' He laughed and turned to walk away. 'And take a long shower. You smell like an old wino.'

'Hey, Alex King. Less of the old.' She snatched up a pillow and slung it at him.

Eleven

Scarlett stayed longer than normal in the shower, soaping herself thoroughly; the last thing she wanted was to have last night's booze still clinging to her when she got to the office. Stepping out and wrapping a towel around her, she leaned her face into the bathroom mirror. She had been told many times that she resembled Taylor Swift but her reflection looked anything but this morning; her skin was sallow and her hazel eyes were slightly bloodshot and watery. She pinched her cheeks to force some colour into them. She'd have to overwork her make up today to freshen up her face.

Returning to the bedroom she dropped the damp towel onto the bed and went to her wardrobe. She selected a light-blue shirt and dark-blue slacks and started to dress. She finished the outfit with a short blue and white striped jumper, leaving the shirt tails hanging below and chose a pair of Vivien Westwood ballet pumps. Yes, they were expensive, she thought as she turned a heel and eyed them, but they were the most comfortable pairs of shoes she had other than her motorcycle boots and trainers and she couldn't go to work in those.

After applying make-up, she made her bed quickly, checked her appearance again in the mirror and headed downstairs. Alex was in the kitchen, wiping down the work surface. He had shaved, waxed his hair and was dressed smartly in an open-necked pinstripe shirt tucked into a pair of jeans.

Eyeing his tight backside, Scarlett felt herself go all goose-bumps. He looked gorgeous.

'Wow, what a transformation,' he said, taking her cup and plate and putting them in the dishwasher.

'You look quite smart yourself, going somewhere?'

'I've got a meeting later this morning.'

'Anything you can talk about?' Alex had been in Military Intelligence but now worked as a consultant in security. Or at least that's what he told her, but whenever she had asked him about his work he changed the subject. Once she'd asked him if he worked for the security services but he had just grinned.

'Now you know if I tell you I'll have to kill you.'

She gently punched his arm and pushed past him, catching a whiff of his aftershave as she picked up her BlackBerry. It brought back memories. She smiled to herself as she checked to see if she'd missed any calls. 'You said you've spoken to Tarn?'

'Yes, told him I was dropping you off. He asked me how you were, said you were a bit down last night when you left work. You said you'd had a shit day. Want to talk about it?'

Scarlett dropped her phone into her bag and faced him. She told him about what had happened to Claudette Jackson and the repercussions for her case – that James Green had been freed.

'Oh, I'm sorry Scarlett.' He gently touched her arm. 'I remember you telling me all about that job. You worked hard on that case.' Then, he said, 'What's that mean now? Is that the end of it? No more trial?'

'No more trial but that's not the end of it. I'm not letting this rest. I'm gunning for James Green. There'll be a review this morning and I'm going to propose we put an operation together to get him.'

Alex snatched up his car keys. 'Well we'd better get you into work then while you're still fired up.'

Twelve

Alex pulled up outside Sutton Police Station and Scarlett gathered her bag from the footwell, leant across and kissed him on the cheek, opened the passenger door and climbed out. Before closing the door she flashed him a smile, thanked him for the lift and promised to text him and give him a call later in the week. As she watched his Range Rover Sport drive away another happy memory of him sprang inside her head and she couldn't help but grin.

Feeling lifted, she walked briskly into the station, swiped her card through the security lock and skipped her way up the stairs to the first floor where The Homicide and Serious Crime Unit were based. But before going in to the office she headed to the ladies to check her appearance again. Satisfied with the way she looked, she headed down the corridor, framing her thoughts on how she was going to address the previous day's disaster. As she approached Detective Inspector Hayden Taylor-Butler's office she saw that his door was open. *The last person I need to see right now.* Being in his presence still filled her with dread. The day at DS Gary Ashdown's barbecue when he had pinched her bum and promised her he could get her promotion regularly messed with her head. Scarlett slowed, breathed in deeply and upped her pace to speed past the opening, deliberately avoiding a look inside his room. Two steps beyond, believing she was safe, she released her breath in a sigh of relief.

Too soon. 'DS Macey.'

Her whole body sagged. She hated the way he said her name: always so condescending. Biting her lip, she spun around and returned to his doorway. The DI's office was small and narrow and most of it was taken up by his huge desk. He was sitting behind it, staring over the top of his reading glasses at her. Easing back in his chair he beckoned her in. There were two additional chairs in the office, up against a wall but he never offered her one.

She stood in front of his desk trying her best not to look as if she didn't want to be here. Butterflies were taking off in her still sensitive stomach. Avoiding eye contact she settled her gaze on his balding head. A curtain of closely-cut greying hair ran around it, making him look older than his 42 years.

Removing his spectacles slowly, Hayden Taylor-Butler set them down on his paperwork. 'I've had the press on to me.'

She returned a questioning look, unsure where this conversation was going.

'Claudette Jackson's mother is threatening to sue us. She's alleging the police are responsible for her daughter's suicide.' He stared at her, narrowing his eyes before continuing. 'She's saying that *you* put pressure on her daughter to give evidence when *you* especially knew how vulnerable she was.'

'That's nonsense.'

'She's made a formal complaint. Professional Standards have rung me this morning. They want to interview you.'

Scarlett's stomach flipped. An inquiry! Weeks of probing. Every aspect of her investigation into the capture of James Green scrutinised by a team of detectives who had gone over to the dark side. Professional Standards was the department's latest name change, the previous one being Complaints and Discipline. The new title was softer, though the job they did was no different. Cops feared them. She answered, 'Claudette wanted to give evidence against Green. I spent a lot of time with her making sure she knew what was required.' She pointed at the paperwork in front of him. She couldn't see her report but she guessed it was somewhere in the pile. 'I put it in her death report. I've listed the times and dates I contacted her. I even made special visits to her to see for myself how she was coping. I gave her every bit of support that I could, and more.'

'That may be the case DS Macey, but once a complaint has been made it has to be thoroughly investigated. They will be looking to make sure you have complied correctly with all procedures, not just in relation to Claudette Jackson's evidence and the way you dealt with her.'

Scarlett scrutinised the look he was giving her. She thought she caught one corner of his mouth lift before returning a deadpan gaze. *He's getting off on this.* Hatred burned within her. She knew he despised her, but she wasn't going to let him see he was getting to her again. Taking a deep breath, she said, 'If you are alluding to what happened at court yesterday – it wasn't my fault. The decision not to prosecute James Green and set him free was not mine. It was CPS's.' Snatching another breath, she added, 'Look I didn't want this to happen. I never expected this.' Studying his disingenuous gawp, she continued, 'I want to have another crack at Green. He's got away with three rapes at least. He's going to strike again – I know it. I want to catch him – get him bang to rights – make sure he doesn't get away with it again.'

DI Taylor-Butler's eyes widened. He pushed himself forward. 'No, you are not going after James Green, DS Macey. You will keep away from him. You've caused enough damage already and you're under investigation.'

'What do you mean I've caused enough damage? It's James Green who's caused the damage. He's the one who's left two women so traumatised that they can't function properly from one day to the next and it's also down to him that Claudette Jackson has committed suicide. 'She was doing her best to stop her voice from breaking.

'Nevertheless, you have to take some responsibility for this. If you hadn't rushed through the operation in your eagerness to capture him, the evidence against him might have been stronger and James Green would now be locked up in spite of the fact that none of the other women were able to give their evidence.' He added, 'Now read my lips DS Macey, leave James Green alone. That's the last I want to hear of this. Case closed. End of discussion.' Resting his arms on his desk and clenching his hands together he said, 'And now I believe you have a post-mortem to go to.'

Thirteen

As she opened her front door, Scarlett longed for nothing more than a long, hot soak and a relaxing night in front of the telly; even if the viewing was rubbish she didn't mind. She was drained. She'd struggled with her hangover all day and as she leant back against her door to shut it she swore never to get like that again. Having to attend Claudette Jackson's post-mortem hadn't helped. She hated PMs at the best of times, but the hangover made things even worse. Her stomach had roiled all the way through it and on several occasions she'd been in danger of losing what little she'd eaten. It wasn't the sight of Claudette's young body being medically dismembered that had caused her to heave but the smell. It always got to her. It was clinging to her clothes right now. She needed to get out of them, and quick.

Toeing off her shoes, she spotted a small pile of post on the floor. It was just a mix of bills, circulars and a couple of local takeaway flyers and with a sigh she scooped them all up, dropped them onto the hall table and skipped upstairs, pulling off her jumper as she went.

Half an hour later, having removed her make-up and stayed longer than normal in the bath – topping it up three times with hot water – she slipped on a T-shirt and pair of leggings and made her way back downstairs, picking her mail back up before heading into the kitchen to prepare herself some food. Her galley kitchen was not big but it was well laid out and organised. Opening the fridge, she checked she had enough salad and then took out a lasagne-for-one from the freezer and popped it into the oven. Setting the timer, she poured a glass of chilled water and began dealing with the post. After binning the flyers, she was left with three envelopes, all bills. She opened the first – council tax. She saw the amount and sighed. She was so grateful she was in a department that regularly had overtime. Under normal circumstances she would never have been able to live in this house on her wage – Richmond upon Thames was where the wealthy lived and the current value of her house was £650,000 – but the two-bedroom, early Victorian, end terrace with patio garden had been bequeathed to her after her Aunt Hanna had lost her battle with leukaemia five years ago. Her younger sister Rose had joint ownership, but she'd only been there twice since Scarlett had tracked her down to a squat four months ago, and that had only been for a few days. The last time they had been together Rose had said she would rather live in squats with her friends who were a friendly bunch of buskers and street artists. It meant that most of the time Scarlett had the place to herself.

She finished opening her mail – the dual fuel bill and water bill – set them aside and prepared herself a larger than normal salad; she was suddenly starving. Adding the cooked lasagne, she took her plate through to the lounge, switched on the TV and plonked herself down on the sofa.

By 9.30 p.m. she'd had enough – she was fighting to keep her eyes open and so she put her dirty plate into the dishwasher, headed upstairs, brushed her teeth and flopped into bed. But, exhausted as she was, Scarlett couldn't fall asleep. As she lay there her head started filling with the past two days of mayhem. Today, especially, had touched her and as she fought to clear her head, flashbacks started invading her brain. She mulled over Claudette's interview, things she'd said that Scarlett had listened to time and time again while preparing for the trial; *'I just lay there. Frozen! …I didn't know what to do! …I can just remember it was cold and wet and all I could think was I hope he'll finish soon so I can get back to my room.'* As she remembered Claudette's words, Scarlett decided that there was no way James Green was going to evade justice. In spite of DI Taylor-Butler's orders she was going after him. She owed it not only to Claudette but also to his other victims.

Fourteen

It had been almost midnight before she finally dropped off but Scarlett strolled into the office feeling refreshed and buoyant. Other than Tarn at his desk, no one else was in. She gazed around the room, stopping at the clock on the wall, checking the time. This was unusual; generally, at this time of day the department was buzzing with activity, the squad fuelling up on coffee and going through their emails before they started their day. Her gaze returned to her partner. She was pleased the office was empty – she wanted to air her plan with him and see if he would go along with it.

Tarn looked up as she scooted back her chair.

'Morning,' she said brightly.

'Morning.'

His response seemed laboured, almost strained. Scarlett studied his face. He looked tired. She was about to ask if he was all right when he said, 'How was Claudette's PM? Was it an overdose?'

Scarlett set down her bag. 'Looks that way. It's not shown anything suspicious anyway. I'm waiting for the toxicology results to confirm everything.'

'Sad.'

'Very sad. That James Green has a lot to answer for.' Scarlett pointed around the room. 'Where is everyone? Am I missing something?'

'Syndicate Two came in early. They're dealing with a couple of stabbings at Streatham – a fight outside a takeaway – one dead and two in hospital. It looks like gang on gang. And George and Ella have gone to a domestic murder at Thornton Heath. A pretty nasty one according to the incident log – bloke took a machete to his partner – almost took off her head. There's a history – the guy's already done time for beating her.'

Scarlett shook her head sadly. 'Why do these women take them back? They get hiding after hiding but still put up with it. It defeats me it does.' She slipped off her jacket and was about to ask him if he wanted a coffee when DI Taylor-Butler walked into the office. She stiffened.

'Don't take your jacket off DS Macey,' he said. 'There's a suspicious death on the Winstanley Estate. Two-year-old boy. Paramedics called it in an hour ago and Uniform are on site. Mother's known to us.' He dropped a print-out from the incident log onto her desk and stabbed a finger at it. 'Details are all in there, including the address. It's already on Facebook and Twitter so I don't know what your reception's going to be. You know what that estate is like. That should keep you out of trouble for a few hours.' Without waiting for a response, he turned to leave, calling back over his shoulder, 'I'm going into morning briefing and then I have a couple of meetings, so you won't be able to get me until after lunch.' Scarlett watched his departure, a shudder running up her spine. She picked up the incident log and began silently reading, feeling herself getting tense. The Winstanley Estate in Wandsworth was one of their most notorious manors; stabbings, robbery and drug dealing were rife. It had been listed as one of Britain's worst places to grow up in. 'Victim's name is Rees Tornese, just two years old, like the gaffer says,' Scarlett read aloud from the report. 'Ambulance service took a 999 call at 7.03 this morning from the mother that her child wasn't breathing. Paramedics got there and found the boy dead in bed. There are some unexplained head injuries so they called in the police. Uniform have secured the scene.' Pausing momentarily to skip-read the time-line she added, 'Mother's name is Kerrie Tornese, twenty-four. She's got a couple for shoplifting and one for possession of class A. Registered with the Public Protection Unit for domestic violence.' Picking up her bag she folded the log and dropped it inside. Then, pulling her jacket back on she glanced across at Tarn. He was gathering his paperwork together. 'Come on, you drive,' she said, heading for the door.

***

They took a pool car. Tarn activated the locks and Scarlett pulled open the passenger door. The stench hit her; stale burgers and fries. The empty food cartons were still in the footwell. 'The lazy bastards,' she said, leaning in and scooping them up. She spotted a couple of chocolate bar wrappers stuffed into the centre consul compartment and picked out those as well. 'I bet this is Carl and Shawn, they've got previous.' She threw the rubbish into a nearby bin, wiped her hands to rid herself of any dirt and picked the log book out from the door slot to check who last used the vehicle. She saw DC Jenkins' signature. 'I was friggin' right, it is Carl. Well he's got a bollocking coming when we get back.' She dropped the log book back into place, checked the front seat to ensure it was clear of any detritus and slid into it. 'That's just sheer idleness, that is. What does it take to throw away your rubbish?'

'You're being anal again.'

'I'm not being anal. What effort does it take to throw away a bit of rubbish? Nothing.' She glanced at Tarn as he started the engine. His face was so serious. *Not the same sparkle to him this morning.* She changed the conversation, 'Is something the matter?'

'Nope.'

His answer was brusque and she studied him for a second. He was staring out through the windscreen, in no rush to move away. She said, 'There is, isn't there?'

Silence reigned between them for several seconds before Tarn responded, 'I think Trish is seeing someone.' He remained staring out through the window as if afraid to look at her.

For a couple of seconds Scarlett was stunned. She caught Tarn's eyes moistening. They had been partners since 2009. She thought she knew everything about him so his reply hit her like a bombshell. For a moment she fought for something to say. Then, she said, 'Trish seeing someone! No, I can't believe that. Not Trish. Are you sure?'

He shook his head. 'I'm not a hundred per cent but there are just a lot of things that are pointing to it.'

'Like what?'

'She's been staying at work a lot just lately. Regularly until eight o'clock. There're a couple of times she's come home smelling of drink and when I've asked her about it she's said a couple of them popped into the pub to wind down. She told me they've had to do a lot of preparation work for an OFSTED visit.'

'Well that could be right.'

He nodded. 'I know, but it's just that she's not been fussed before about them. Usually she's brought the work home. And a couple of weeks ago she went away on a teacher's conference – Friday and Saturday. She's never done that. She's always said she's glad to get away from the classroom and teachers – especially when it was my weekend off.'

Scarlett processed what Tarn had told her. After a few seconds she said, 'That's not enough to accuse her of seeing someone. Come on, think about it. This is Trish you're talking about.'

His mouth tightened. 'I know. I've done nothing else but think about it. But these last few months I've seen changes in her and they coincide with the new head that's come. I've met him a couple of times and he's quite a likeable guy. A mate told me he'd seen them in the pub one of the times after she told me she'd been working late.'

'That doesn't mean she's seeing him, Tarn. You and I go to the pub together after work.'

'Yes, but I always tell Trish. That's what we do. She's never done that. When they break up – yes – a group of them go out to celebrate the end of term. But not midweek, after work. And why tell me she was working late when she was really down the pub with him?'

Scarlett again considered what her partner had just said. 'Have you challenged her about what your mate saw?'

He turned, 'No. I didn't know how to broach it. I didn't want her to think I'd been spying on her... I guess I'm afraid of what her answer will be.'

Scarlett saw the grief in his face. 'I've already said this, but this is Trish you're speaking about. *You* and Trish. Two wonderful kids together, *You* and Trish. When I think about all the other guys in the office and the state of their marriages, *Yours* and Trish's is probably one of the most solid ones I know.'

'You think I'm just being silly.'

'This job always puts a strain on marriages, you know that! And you've said yourself that Trish is under pressure, working long hours for this OFSTED visit. What you two need is a break.' She held his gaze. 'And if you need Auntie Scarlett to look after Dale and Heather, no problemo.'

'You have Dale and Heather for a couple of days? No thank you! The last thing they need to learn is your life skills. They've got enough bad habits as it is!' Tarn's solemn face broke into a grin.

She punched his arm. 'Daft sod. Now come on, we've got a job to go to.'

Fifteen

They swung into the Winstanley Estate. The place was made up of drab grey monoliths of concrete from the 60s and 70s. Scarlett took one look at the first block they passed and wondered who on earth would want to live in such a neglected looking place. She wasn't surprised the young people revolted from time to time. Up ahead, by one of the low-rise blocks, a group had formed outside the entrance. Three cops in high-visibility jackets were doing their best to keep them in check. Beyond, Scarlett spotted a line of emergency vehicles parked up and pointed them out to Tarn.

Slowing, he steered carefully around the assembled residents, many of whom turned and noseyed as they passed, and pulled up behind a CSI van. The block they parked beside was one of the newer builds, comprising three storeys with interconnecting corridors.

Scarlett got out of the car and went to the boot, removed her jacket, dropped it inside and pulled on a protective all-in-one. As she watched Tarn slip on plastic overshoes she glanced about her. The crowd around the block entrance was about thirty strong. A mix of ages. Half-a-dozen youths, no older than fourteen, were circling nearby on their BMXs. Some were stood up rigid on their pedals, weaving slowly, watching. She guessed they were the estate 'dickers' for the drug dealers, ready to fly off should circumstances demand it. She switched her attention back to the assembly and wondered if anyone knew anything. She'd give the uniform officers corralling the crowd the job of taking down names. That thought momentarily made her smile. She wondered how many of the onlookers would be willing to assist.

Probably none, given the estate's reputation. Slipping on her lanyard identification she checked Tarn was okay to go and led the way to the block's entrance. As she approached the nearest officer she held out her ID. His young-looking face told her he'd rather be somewhere else.

'Where is everyone?' she asked.

He tipped his head upwards, 'Second floor. Flat twenty-three.'

With a smile, she instructed him to find out if anyone in the crowd had any information and then headed for the entrance. The large foyer with metal and concrete staircase was full of graffiti but smelt as if it had been recently cleaned. A slim, dark haired female officer was on guard here. Again, Scarlett held out her ID for scrutiny. The young policewoman checked it and pointed them up the stairs. 'It's flat twenty-three. My Sergeant's up there with CSI who've just turned up.'

'What about the Mother?' Scarlett had forgotten the woman's name. The incident log was still in her bag so she fished it out to refresh herself.

'They've taken her back to Battersea.'

'Has she been arrested?'

'No just PACE nine.'

That technically meant mum was there as a volunteer and not under arrest. However, in reality she would be prevented from leaving until she at least had given an account of this morning's discovery.

'So the scene is secure?'

The officer nodded.

'Good.' Scarlett climbed the stairs with Tarn close behind. On the second floor landing she bunched her hair inside her hood and slipped on latex gloves. She spotted another uniformed officer standing by an open door, half way along the landing. He was holding a clipboard and looking their way, pen poised as they approached.

Once more flashing her ID Scarlett announced who they were, and as the log officer scribbled down their names and noted the time, she and Tarn stepped into the flat.

Sixteen

The foul stench that greeted Scarlett made her gasp. It shouldn't have come as a surprise given the sight before her; waist-high rubbish was strewn the length of the hallway. She shot a look back at Tarn, shook her head in disgust and began negotiating her way past piles of full black bin bags, some of which had burst, spilling out their contents of rotted food and discarded containers. There were small mounds of soiled children's clothing, empty beer cans and faeces to avoid before she got to the bottom of the stairs. Muffled voices were coming from above.

She called up and a hooded and masked head appeared over the balcony.

'DS Macey and DC Scarr from Homicide and Serious Crime.'

The man stepped into the open and pulled down his protective face-mask. 'Sergeant Harrison from Battersea. I was first on scene with PC Stewart who's doing the visitor log.'

'What have we got?' Scarlett began her climb up the stairs.

'The woman who lives here is Kerrie Tornese. She called the ambulance service just after seven this morning saying she'd just found her son, two-year-old Rees, unconscious and she thought he was dead. Paramedics got here less than ten minutes later and found him dead in his bed. Kerrie told them she last checked him just after ten last night and he was alive but they're not happy with that explanation. It's their opinion he's been dead for a lot longer than nine hours. And there are a number of unexplained bruises on the child's body. The two paramedics are waiting in the ambulance – I've told them we'll need a statement before they leave.'

Reaching the landing, Scarlett made a mental note of what the Sergeant had told her. 'You sound as though you know Kerrie. Is that right?'

'Yes, I know Kerrie very well. I nicked her as a teenager for shoplifting and possession. She's been a junkie for as long as I've known her. Before that she was always running away from home. She's had this gaff for a good few years. I've been to a couple of domestics here during the past eighteen months. She was living with a well-known dealer called Darrell Stringer until last summer when he was lifted by Drug Squad with a load of gear on him. He's serving three years in Pentonville for supplying. We believe Rees is his kid.'

'What about Rees. Do you know anything about him?'

'All I know is what Kerrie told us when we got here – that he's two. I haven't been able to do any checks to see if he's on the 'at-risk'.''

'Okay. What about Kerrie. Has she said much else about what happened?'

'No. Only told us what she'd told the paramedics. She's not very communicative. She stank of booze and she was spaced out when I got here. Looks as though she's still on the smack, given the amount of needles around.'

'What's happening with Rees?'

'CSI are in with the body now. We're just waiting for the pathologist to get here.'

'Okay, great. Anything else I need to know?'

He shook his head, then added, 'She's got a little girl. I can't remember her name. I can remember seeing her when I came to the last domestic. She's five, maybe six. She doesn't appear to be here. Kerrie's mother doesn't live too far away so she might be with her.'

A bedroom door opened and out stepped a well-made man in a tightly-fitting forensic suit.

Scarlett recognised who it was even before he'd fully removed his mask. 'Mason Gregory, well fancy meeting you here.' Mason was one of the very few detectives who specialised in forensics, most being civilians, and was a CSI Supervisor, who took on a regular role of Crime Scene Manager. In years past he had worked alongside her father in CID. The last time she had seen

Mason was four months ago, by the banks of the Thames near Ham House. He was examining a suspect vehicle in a murder case she was working on: that case that had resulted in her finding Rose and had finally cleared her sister as a suspect in their parent's murder.

'I thought I heard your dulcet tones Detective Sergeant Macey,' he smiled. 'How are you?'

'Really good thank you. Well I was until I got here. This is a real shit-hole.'

'Believe it or not I've been in worse places, though this is a close call.'

Scarlett jerked her head towards the bedroom he'd come from. 'I know I can't go in there yet, but is there anything you can tell me?'

'The boy's in bed. Certainly been dead a fair bit of time, although we'll not know for definite until the pathologist gets here. The kid looks badly malnourished to me and there are a number of bruises on his torso. Chest and arms especially. There are a couple on his head and there's a strange mark on his neck that we can't fathom out at the moment.'

Scarlett's brow furrowed. 'What do you mean?'

'It's like a band that goes all the way round. I've photographed it, as well as all the bruises on the rest of his body and swabbed the skin. Once the body is removed to the mortuary we'll put him through the scanner to see what that brings up.'

'Okay, that's smashing Mason. Do you mind if I have a look round?'

'Be my guest, but don't rummage around too much, I need to photograph and examine the rest of the place.'

'No, I won't. I just want to view the rooms, that's all.'

Mason put his mask back in place, gave her an okay hand signal and went back into the bedroom.

Scarlett turned to Tarn and the Sergeant, 'Can you two see what we've got downstairs? I'll just give the bathroom and this other bedroom the once over and then we'll convene back in the hallway and wait for the pathologist to arrive.'

As Tarn and the Sergeant went downstairs she headed into the bathroom. She pushed the door open but only poked her head around before determining she didn't want to go any further. It stank. The toilet hadn't been flushed, there was shit smeared around the bath and the sink was full of dirty nappies. She screwed up her nose and stepped back outside, shutting the door. Passing the room where Rees lay dead, she walked to the front bedroom. The finger-smeared door was ajar and she opened it fully. It was sticky to the touch. The mess in this room and the smell were no better. Discarded clothing cluttered the floor, fighting for space with empty vodka bottles and foreign lager cans. Used syringes and other drug paraphernalia littered a bedside cabinet. The double bed was heavily stained with what looked like urine. This looked to be Kerrie's room. Scarlett was about to leave when she heard a rustling noise. It sounded as if it was coming from beneath the bed. Her stomach tightened as she called 'Who's there? Come out from beneath the bed now!' For a moment, there was silence. Scarlett strained her ears. A sudden shuffling noise was followed by a shadow snaking its way out from beneath the mattress. Then a head appeared, followed by small hands and arms clutching a teddy bear. It was a little girl. Cowering in semi darkness. She looked terrified. Scarlett's racing heart began to slow as relief washed over her. 'Hello,' she said gently. The little girl's large brown eyes just stared. Scarlett squatted down and pulled back her suit hood to reveal more of her face. This called for a comforting approach. 'I'm Scarlett. What's your name?'

There was a good ten seconds silence as the girl looked her over, before she said, 'Ruby.'

'Hello Ruby. What are you doing under there? Hiding?'

The little girl nodded.

'Who are you hiding from?'

'Mummy.'

Scarlett felt a sudden rush of adrenalin. 'Why are you hiding from mummy?'

'She was mad.'

'Mad with you?'

'No. Mad with Rees.'

'Why was she mad with Rees?'

'He wouldn't stop crying. He dropped and broke the cup of water I gave him. Mummy shouted and hit him but he wouldn't stop crying so she took him upstairs to lock him in the bedroom. I hid because she was very mad.'

'Well your mummy's not here now. We've come to look after you.' Scarlett held out a hand to Ruby. 'Do you want to come out from under there and see what present I've got for you?'

Ruby released one grubby hand from her teddy bear and stretched it out toward her. 'Rees isn't crying any more. Have you given him a present?'

Seventeen

Scarlett led Ruby carefully downstairs by the hand, meeting Tarn at the bottom. He couldn't hide his surprise as he looked from the girl to Scarlett and back.

'This is Ruby. She's six, and this is Freddy her teddy. I found them hiding under the bed because they're scared of mummy, didn't I Ruby?' she said, looking down at the child. Her hair was matted and her pyjamas didn't look as though they had been washed for weeks. Scarlett thought that she probably had head lice and shuddered. If Alex, or anyone else rang her tonight she really would be telling them she was staying in and washing her hair.

The little girl gazed up uncertainly at Tarn and nodded, her mouth set tight.

'Well my name's Tarn and I work with Scarlett. I'm very pleased to meet you and Freddy.'

The little girl's hesitant expression broke. She giggled. 'Freddy's not real, he's only a teddy.'

Squeezing her hand gently Scarlett said, 'Me and Ruby are going to go back to where I work and play some games and I'm going to show her all the dolls we have, aren't I?' She lifted her eyes away from Ruby, fixing Tarn with a serious look. In a half-whisper she continued, 'I'm going to get the paramedics to give her a quick once-over and check she's okay, and then I'm going to take her to the Interview Suite and get the FME and Social Services out. I need to get something recorded while she's talking freely.'

He nodded, 'Okay. What do you need me to do?'

'You wait here for the pathologist, see what the initial findings are and then oversee the removal of the body. Also see what evidence Mason's found. I'm especially interested in that banding mark he mentioned around the lad's neck.' She started unzipping her suit. She didn't want to take the girl back to the car wearing her forensic suit. It wouldn't look right going past the residents dressed like that while holding Ruby's hand. Climbing out of her suit she handed it to Tarn for him to bag as an exhibit, then, re-taking Ruby's hand she said, ' Right Ruby, what do you say to some pop and sweets before we go and play with some dolls?'

Ruby looked up with an excited smile, 'Ooh yes please.'

Scarlett blinked away a tear. Giving the little girl's hand another reassuring squeeze, she set off.

***

Outside, the crowd had swelled by a dozen or so while she had been in the flat but it was orderly. All eyes set on her as she stepped out of the entranceway. Stooping, Scarlett said quietly, 'My car's just down here Ruby. But before we go to play with the dolls I'm going to take you to a couple of friends of mine who are in that ambulance over there. They're going to have a quick look to see that mummy's not hurt you.'

Ruby looked up, 'She hasn't because I don't cry like Rees. She only gets mad with him 'cos he cries a lot.'

'Well I'd still like you to meet them. Is that okay?'

Ruby nodded.

Out of the corner of her eye, Scarlett caught a sudden flash to her right. Someone was taking a photo. She stopped mid-stride, spun around and rapidly scanned the crowd. She caught sight of someone pulling away a mobile from their face and dodging out of sight. Her heart lurched. The glimpse of the young man's face was only fleeting but in that split-second she recognised who it was. She searched among the heads to where she'd seen him duck but he was nowhere to be seen. Her heart was banging against her chest. She was certain it was James Green.

Eighteen

Scarlett stopped the video footage and ejected the disc from the computer. With an overwhelming sense of anger, she turned to Tarn sitting beside her. As if reading her thoughts, he shook his head in disgust. They had just finished watching the interview with Ruby Tornese. The female detective conducting it had performed a masterful piece of discussion with the six-year-old, and while it had been priceless in terms of evidence gathering it had also been heart-breaking to watch; several times, Scarlett felt a lump rising in her throat and had to swallow hard. The little girl had talked about her two-year-old brother being smacked and punched by her mum as if that was the norm. The cruelty Ruby had witnessed on a daily basis was beyond comprehension; she'd seen him being hit regularly with 'mummy's belt' and then locked in the cupboard under the stairs while they went to the shops, and she'd also described how she had 'watched mummy put the 'buzzy' collar around Rees's neck, when she was really angry with him.' She said, 'Rees wet himself when mummy did that': they had found an electric dog training collar hidden in the bottom of the kitchen waste bin; it matched the mark around Rees's neck: As if punching and belting her son hadn't been enough, Kerrie had tortured him with electric shocks for fun.

Ruby had left the station with a social worker and was now with temporary foster parents. It wasn't ideal, but at least her life was going to get better from now on. Not so for her little brother. His life was over. That afternoon Scarlett had gone to Rees Tornese's post-mortem. It had been one of the most harrowing PMs she'd ever attended. A couple of times she'd felt she was going to lose it and she'd had to fight hard to mask her emotions. When Scarlett had first seen his naked body laid out on the metal gurney, she had frozen, stunned by the frailness of his body. Just as quickly though, she had switched into investigation mode, processing his torso as evidence rather than a person – something she had to do to get the job done. The two-and-a-half-hour autopsy had revealed Rees was badly malnourished, had scabies and forty-six injuries over the length and breadth of his body. Most of the bruising had been caused by punching, some by a belt; the buckle mark was still evident on his skin. His death had been caused by a bleed to the brain; he had been repeatedly thumped in the head. The Pathologist had also determined that Rees had been dead for between 15 and 20 hours, so couldn't have been alive at 10 o'clock last night as Kerrie had told them.

They had interviewed Kerrie twice – she'd needed a break because of the withdrawal shakes and a doctor had been called – but neither of those interrogations had got to the truth of what she'd done. She had lied through her teeth. Her continued response was that Rees was accident prone – always bumping into things and banging his head and she even had the impudence to say that Ruby sometimes played rough with him. There was no sadness, no remorse in her answers, just a blame game, and she wasn't the one to blame. There had been a few moments during the questioning when Scarlett had felt the urge to inflict some physical pain upon Kerry but she had clenched her hands beneath the table that thankfully separated them, and kept them there until the interview had ended.   *How the fuck could a mother do that to their child? The Bitch.*

'Well I thought I was tough, but I could weep for those two kids,' said Tarn. 'I mean, what kind of life did they have? Especially poor Rees. Someone like that doesn't deserve to have kids.'

Scarlett placed the DVD into its box and started filling out the evidence label. 'She'll get what's coming to her on remand. No one likes a child killer. Not even prisoners.' Slipping the DVD into her top drawer she checked her watch. 'Talking about kids, haven't you got a home to go to?'

Tarn checked his own watch, 'We've got the rest of the evidence to book in and the charges to do yet.'

'I can sort that. It's only an hour's work. We'll do the remand file tomorrow. Kerrie Tornese is not going anywhere, is she? And anyway, sorting out your marriage is more important than this.'

'To be honest Scarlett I could do with getting off. Trish has been playing on my mind all day.'

'You get yourself off and I'll finish off here.'

'You sure?'

'Absolutely. See you tomorrow.'

Tarn didn't bother tidying his desk like he usually did. He locked his drawers, dragged his coat off the back of his chair and headed for the door.

Scarlett watched him go with a heavy heart. She'd been watching him all day. He'd gone about his job like the professional he was, but without his usual bounce and enthusiasm. She hoped her partner had got it wrong about his wife having an affair. She'd seen too many of her colleagues' marriages go to the wall. She tried to convince herself that was one of the reasons why she'd stayed single.

Nineteen

It was almost 10 p.m. by the time Scarlett clocked off and eleven by the time she got home. She stripped off her clothes in the kitchen and dumped them in the washing machine and then climbed wearily up the stairs to the bathroom where she turned on the shower. Turning it up a couple of notches she stepped into the hot cascade. For a few seconds it felt like the water was piercing her skin and then she got used to it and tilted back her head, closing her eyes. The image of Rees Tornese's frail and battered body lying on the autopsy gurney had cemented itself to her inner vision since the post-mortem that afternoon and she hadn't been able to unhook it. The sight of the blonde haired, skinny boy, lying dead on that cold metal examination table, his angrily-bruised flesh stretched over chicken-thin bones was going to stay with her for a very long time. Probably for ever.

Before she left work, Scarlett had charged Kerrie with murder and it was the first time Scarlett had seen the hardness in Kerrie's face crack. The moment she'd been asked if she wanted to make a reply to the charge Kerrie had broken down. She'd screamed like a banshee and collapsed to the floor. Scarlett had walked away without any feeling of pity. In fact as she'd slammed the cell door shut, her only thought was that Kerrie should suffer the same hell in prison as Rees had. Now there were other things on her mind as she opened her eyes – scabies and head-lice. She reached for the shower soap and scrubbed her arms until they were red.

Twenty minutes later, in her dressing gown, she headed into the kitchen. She was famished. In the fridge, she found a pasta salad she'd bought two days ago – it was still in date – and poured herself a glass of white wine; she needed to come down after the day she'd had. Then, she went into the lounge, switched on the TV and dumped herself down on the sofa. Swallowing a decent slug of wine she set down her glass on the coffee table, picked up her salad and the TV remote and began surfing the channels. She found an episode of *Friends* that she'd seen a couple of times but didn't care – she needed something that wouldn't tax her mashed up brain.

Settling back against the scatter cushions, she dug into her pasta salad and had just forked in a mouthful when the flash of that afternoon's event – the person photographing her with their mobile – entered her mind's eye. It had visited her a few times throughout the day but she had been so tied up with things that she'd pushed it aside. Now it had popped up again and wasn't going away until she'd resolved it. She stopped chewing and closed her eyes, willing the image to return but her brain was having none of it. She had been convinced at the time that it was James Green she had seen but the reflection was so distant now she wasn't so confident. Besides, Green lived in a flat in Twickenham. Why would he be across in the Winstanley Estate? Just then something more disturbing entered her thinking – had he taken to following her?

Twenty

The next morning, after another disturbed night's sleep, Scarlett had just stepped out of the shower when the front doorbell sounded. Confused, wondering who it could be because it was too early for the postman, she slung on her dressing gown and, still wet, trotted downstairs to answer the door. It was Tarn and he looked forlorn. Stepping back to usher him in, she said, 'That look on your face tells me it didn't go well between you and Trish last night?'

He closed the door. 'She wouldn't even discuss it.'

'What happened?'

'I waited while the kids went to bed and then put it to her that things didn't seem right with her. She wouldn't answer so I asked her if she was seeing someone.'

'What did she say?'

'Just laughed at me. She said I was being ridiculous. When I told her she'd been seen in the pub with Adam – that's the new head - she said they'd gone there after work for a drink. That it was no big deal.'

'That's what I said, didn't I?'

'Her face said otherwise. I could tell she wasn't being honest with me. She's not a good liar, so I said straight out that I thought she was seeing Adam.'

'And I guess it didn't go down too well?'

'Not at all. She said if that was what I thought then there was no point in talking about it. I asked her to just be honest with me but she said she didn't want to talk about it.' He flung up his arms in dismay. 'And that was it. She went up to bed. When I went up half an hour later she pretended to be asleep. I haven't slept a wink.'

'I don't know what to say Tarn. I'm sorry it's not turning out for you. I'd offer to speak to Trish, but I don't know her well enough to have a heart-to-heart with her.'

'Thanks Scarlett, but it's not your problem. It's mine and Trish's to sort out.'

Scarlett, gently stroked his arm and offered a reassuring smile. 'Feel okay for work? If you don't, you can always throw a sickie. It would give you some time with Trish. That's more important.'

'No point. She's in work this morning. Anyway, we've got a couple of days off after today haven't we? It'll give me time over the weekend. I'm going to see if my mum and dad will have the kids to give us some time together.' After a moment, he continued, 'And we've got a remand file to do this morning for Kerrie Tornese.'

'I can do that. That's the least of your worries.'

'No, I'd rather get my head down. It might help divert some of my thoughts.'

'Okay, but if at any time you need to be away just say the word.'

'Thanks Scarlett. I might take you up on getting a flyer if nothing else happens.'

'No problem.' Turning back to the stairs she said, 'And now, partner, I have my work face to put on. Stick the kettle on and make us a coffee and I'll be down in ten.'

'Can I make some toast as well? I'm starving. I haven't eaten this morning.'

'Sure,' she replied, beginning her ascent. 'Put me a slice in as well. You'll find half a loaf in the bottom of the freezer.' As she headed into her bedroom she thought of James Green again. She'd wanted to tell Tarn about yesterday but now wasn't the time. Her partner had more pressing problems to worry about.

Twenty-one

In the squad room Scarlett booted up her computer, toe-flicked off her shoes beneath her desk and started work on the remand file. She sent Tarn to get them a coffee from the canteen and when he returned she tasked him with chasing up statements from witnesses; primarily they needed evidence from the paramedics who had found Rees's body, and the Sergeant and PC who had been first on scene, for that afternoon's hearing, but long term they would need written testimonies from the pathologist and CSI officers for when the case went to Crown Court. Scarlett also needed to contact Social Services. That morning a note had been waiting on her desk informing her that both Ruby and Rees were on the At-Risk Register following several case conferences held to discuss the children's plight. She wanted to know what evidence had been presented at those meetings; it could be vital for their case.

Half an hour into her report, Scarlett's concentration was disturbed by loud chatter. She looked up as Detectives George Martin and Ella Bloom appeared. George and Ella were part of her syndicate, working as a team. She hadn't been able to catch up with them these past few days because they had been working on the domestic murder, where the husband had almost hacked off his wife's head.

She met their gaze. 'All sorted?'

'Yep! He's coughed it! We've just charged him.' said George, putting his document folder on his desk. He was red-faced and blowing hard.

Scarlett studied him for a moment. She wasn't surprised he was breathing heavily – George had been steadily gaining weight for the past year and even though he was 6' 7" it was more than was healthy for him. At 51, he was no spring chicken. He was spending less than a quarter of the time at the gym than he used to and yet still putting away the same amount of fast-food and beer. She'd seen it happen to a lot of detectives, which was why she was determined to keep running. In spite of his bulk though, George was no slouch; he could match anyone's work-rate in the Squad. And his knowledge and experience were invaluable. Recently, George primarily had been responsible for nailing her parents' murderers. She said, 'Was it you who got the cough or Ella?'

George shot her an indignant look, 'What are you trying to say Sergeant Macey – that I'm losing my touch? I'll have you know a good detective will always beat charm and beauty.'

Ella's mouth dropped open, 'Ooh George Martin. How could you!' She looked from George to Scarlett. 'Don't you let him kid you – it was a team effort. In fact, it was me who found the murder weapon. He'd put it in a neighbour's bin.'

Scarlett gave a short laugh, 'Well done you two.' She thought about what George had just said. He could not have chosen more appropriate words to describe Ella – she was charming and certainly was beautiful. Ella was slim with short white-blonde hair, dazzling blue eyes, thin nose, and a full mouth and looked a lot younger than her twenty-six years. When Scarlett had first met her, such was her prettiness that one of their first girlie chats had been to ask if she had ever been a model. Ella had laughed, shook her head, and told her she'd had a couple of offers to join agencies, but that she'd wanted to be a policewoman since the age of six, after being invited to a classmate's party and meeting their funny and lovely mother who worked for the British Transport Police.

Ella caught Scarlett's eye and flicked her head towards the door, an hint that she wanted to talk. Scarlett acknowledged her with a quick smile, found her shoes beneath her desk, picked up her bag next to her chair and followed Ella out of the room to the toilets. Ella was standing by the hand basins greeting her with a beaming smile.

'That face tells me you have some exciting news, girl.'

'I think Ryan's going to propose to me this weekend.'

Ella had been dating Ryan Anderson for the best part of eighteen months. He was a detective over in Brixton; they had worked together before Ella got this job. Scarlett had met him twice when he'd come to taxi her and Ella home after a couple of their girl's nights out. He was a nice guy and she'd had that confirmed from several sources. 'Wow Ella, that's fantastic. You got something lined up then?'

'Weekend in Paris. He sprung it on me two nights ago. Right out of the blue.'

'Well girl you need to get some nice underwear then.'

'Tonight's plan,' she giggled.

'I'm so pleased for you. Tell me all about it Monday morning.' Scarlett leaned in and gave her a hug; she was happy for Ella, but strangely, at that moment she experienced a sudden twinge of envy; it was something she had thought about with Alex before she had messed things up between them. As she embraced her friend, Scarlett caught her reflection in the mirror. Although she was smiling, inside there was a wrench of sadness.

Twenty-two

Scarlett awoke refreshed from the best sleep she'd had all week. As she propped herself up in bed, she shooed away thoughts of the previous week. She didn't want another one like that for a long time. She'd left work drained yesterday evening; working on the Kerrie Tornese file had left her mentally worn out, so bushed that all she had wanted was a soak in the bath and chill in front of the TV with a couple of glasses of wine. She couldn't even be bothered to cook and so she'd got a pizza on the way home. Now she was feeling guilty about how much she had eaten – only one slice remained from a 12" pizza. Eyeing the strong sunlight filtering through her curtains she decided to go for a run – a long one at that, not to just burn off last night's pizza, but all the other crap she'd eaten recently. Besides she wanted to look her best for tomorrow; Alex had texted her before she had left work and asked her if she fancied doing Sunday lunch. Thinking about Ella and her weekend in Paris, it had taken her seconds to respond with a 'Yes'.

Swinging her legs out of bed she sprang into action, changing quickly into running gear and jogging downstairs to begin her warm up. After locking the front door, she stretched her hamstrings and calves and took several deep breaths. Then, setting her time on her watch she set off at gentle jog. A hundred yards in, she stepped up the tempo. A quarter of a mile on and she began pushing herself – she knew what time she had to aim for as she chose her longest route, along Richmond Hill, down the Terrace Gardens and out along the towpath beside the Thames towards Ham, where she would turn around and return: it was a good five miles.

By the time she'd reached Petersham Meadows she had settled into a decent pace and her breathing had become regular, but she was feeling uneasy. She'd found herself looking about her the moment she had reached the towpath, and at first she put it down to the job she'd been involved in several months ago – a dismembered body, crammed inside a suitcase, had been found only quarter a mile ahead beside the riverbank. Now though, with each step, she had a sense of being followed. She glanced behind her a couple of times and once she caught sight of a hooded figure running a few hundred yards behind. For a nanosecond James Green popped into her thoughts and that rattled her, but the runner peeled away, heading back into town, and she heaved a sigh of relief, telling herself she was becoming paranoid. The event caused her to slacken her pace. Her watch told her she was a good minute slower than normal so, clawing in a lungful of air, she kicked up her heels and put in a burst.

By the time she got home she had pushed herself so hard that she was shaking and convinced she was going to throw up. Doubling over, supporting herself with one arm against the wall, she took in gulps of air and steadied her breathing, regaining her composure. It took a couple of minutes to recover, then she stretched out and went inside to get some water.

Twenty-three

James Green spotted Scarlett the moment she came out through her gate and onto the footpath. She was wearing a sweat top and tight lycra leggings. He dodged down quickly behind a parked car, pretending to tie his shoelaces, staying there as she stretched out her calves and hamstrings. *Nice arse Detective Macey.*

Seconds later he watched her set off at a jog. He told himself that he would give her a few more seconds before he followed. Seeing her pick up her pace and turn the corner, he noted she was heading towards Sheen Road, towards Richmond Bridge.

Now it was safe to follow.

Turning the corner of her road he was surprised how far ahead she had got. *You're fast Detective Macey.* But he was fast too. He knew he needed to hang back, reminding himself he was following merely to observe; *study your enemy. Know their strengths and weaknesses.* He kept his pace and his distance.

It was as he thought - she was pounding along Sheen Road. But then, after a hundred yards, she took a turn onto Richmond Hill and bombed down the Terrace Gardens and onto the Thames towpath. It took him by surprise and he had to put in a spurt. By the time he hit the footpath beside the river he was clawing for breath. Then he spotted her looking back over her shoulder. Back at him. He was so glad he'd left a good gap between them; there was no way she would be able to see it was *him* following.

Something's spooked her.

He didn't want to blow it. He had plenty of time; he'd already found out where she lived thanks to his patience.

Turning away, he sprinted for home.

Twenty-four

Following a long shower, Scarlett dried her hair, changed into jeans and a thin woollen jumper, lunched on banana and yoghurt and then headed to the High Street to do a big shop; she was running low – not just of food, but of other household items as well. Along the way she couldn't resist paying a visit to a couple of clothes shops, buying a new top, a pair of trousers and some chunky costume jewellery for tomorrow's meet with Alex; it had been a good few months since she had treated herself to something new and she wanted to make a good impression.

Purchases in hand, she made for her original destination – the supermarket. For ten minutes she scoured aisles and shelves, picking up the things she desperately needed, alongside a few treats she didn't, but in that instant fancied. As she selected a piece of filleted salmon from the fish counter a sudden movement at the periphery of her vision brought her up sharp. It was a fleeting glimpse of someone moving fast at the corner of her eye. Turning sharply, she was just in time to see a hooded figure turning into the next food lane. The hoodie the person was wearing was light grey – the same colour as the runner from that morning. Her heart lurched. She dropped the tray of salmon into her trolley and trotted after the figure, but there was no one fitting the description she'd seen. She rushed to the next aisle. Again, there was no one in a grey hooded top. For a brief moment she panned her eyes over much of the store from where she was standing but to no avail. She cursed inwardly, telling herself this was stupid. *She* was being stupid. She'd got James Green too firmly inside her head and she needed to dislodge him *now* and get on with her weekend. She continued with her shopping, though she glanced over her shoulder once or twice, but as she put the last items into her trolley and pushed it towards the till she told herself she was definitely becoming obsessed with Green and allowed herself a half-laugh. Watching the woman in front packing her shopping she began feeding her goods onto the belt for the cashier, mentally ticking off each article she set down against the shopping list she held inside her head. As she set down the last of her items she happened to glance up at the large windows which gave a view out to the car park. And there she saw James Green looking at her from outside, his face pressed against the window, a smug, superior grin etched across his face. He waved at her, and then turned and walked slowly away. A strange sensation overcame her. Some of it was anger but some of it was fear.

Twenty-five

Scarlett took a taxi home. As a precaution she got the driver to drop her off in the next street so she could check if Green had followed her. As the taxi pulled away and she stood with her shopping at her feet, she looked around and could feel the fury building. By the time she had walked the few hundred yards home – checking around every dozen or so steps – she was a melting pot of rage. After opening the front door, she set down her shopping, slammed the door and let out an enormous scream.

He's fucking stalking me! The bastard!

Thirty seconds later, feeling a little calmer, Scarlett carried her bags into the kitchen and began unloading her purchases and putting them away, though she couldn't shake Green's conceited face from her thoughts. She wanted to punch the living daylights out of him. As she stored away the last of her things she considered ringing Tarn to tell him what had happened, but dismissed it; he had his marriage to sort out and he wouldn't appreciate her call. Besides, Green was long gone and nothing could be done right now. She would leave it until Monday and bring it up at briefing. It would give her ammunition to target James Green again.

That afternoon, following lunch of a ham and cucumber sandwich, she threw open a couple of windows, and the French doors to her patio garden, put on the TV's rock music channel, and cleaned the house, changing the sheets on her bed and putting on the washing machine. It felt quite cathartic and by late afternoon she had rid herself of the frustration of what had happened earlier at the supermarket. After a long soak in the bath she prepared an evening meal of a salad with the salmon she had bought that morning, washed down with chilled Sauvignon Blanc. Then, in her dressing gown, she settled down on the sofa to watch TV with the remainder of her wine; it was quite some time since she'd done a quiet Saturday night in, but A, she was still feeling shattered from the week she'd endured, and B, she wanted to feel fresh for tomorrow when she was meeting Alex.

**

Scarlett awoke with a start. A sound had made her jump and she realised it was from the TV. She'd fallen asleep watching *Casualty* but it had ended, replaced by the news; she had only been asleep for twenty minutes. The first thing she spotted was her empty glass and the empty wine bottle; the drink had relaxed her and she'd dropped off; she was more tired than she'd thought. As she sat up a sudden draught at her neck made her shiver. It was coming from the hall. She raised herself off the sofa, feeling a chill about the room. Re-arranging her dressing gown, she pulled it snug and fastened the belt as she stepped into the hall. The draught was stronger here, coming from the kitchen which was in darkness. Switching on the light her gaze fastened upon the French doors to her bijou patio garden. They were open. Wide open. She could have sworn she had closed them before she'd gone for her bath. Then she remembered she'd definitely seen them closed when she'd prepared her evening meal. Suddenly she was unnerved again.

Twenty-six

James Green lay in bed grinning to himself and reflecting on the day's entertainment. First he'd followed Detective Macey out on a run and then on her shopping spree. He knew he shouldn't have, but the adrenalin rush had been so good that he'd not been able to resist waving to her. To let her know *he* was there. Then there had been tonight. That had really capped the day: he had climbed the fence into her garden, found she'd left the French doors into her kitchen unlocked and hadn't been able to resist the opportunity to sneak inside. He had caught her asleep on the sofa. Just yards away. The buzz had been truly spectacular – like nothing else he had ever experienced. He knew he could have done her there and then, but the control he had exerted upon himself had given him an extra surge of adrenalin, spiking him and fulfilling his need for that moment. He had snapped her on his phone and then tiptoed back through her kitchen, letting himself out and climbed back over the fence without her knowing. Now he'd done it once he knew there would be another opportunity. *Detective Macey wouldn't know what was coming.*

James started to play with himself. He was rock hard. The Lycra Rapist had been inside Detective Macey's house without her knowing. This was a cause for celebration.

Twenty-seven

Scarlett had suffered a restless night despite having checked and double-checked every window, double locked the doors and set the perimeter alarm – a first – before going to bed. The incident with the French doors had unnerved her. James Green had tunnelled his way into her thoughts and made her too pumped up to relax. She had told herself that she was being ridiculous – she was stretching her imagination too far – there was a simple solution to this; she'd closed the doors, but she hadn't locked them and the breeze had blown them open. In spite of repeatedly telling herself this, she had not managed to convince herself and she'd lain awake well into the early hours latching onto every sound around her, no matter how slight. When she had finally succumbed to sleep it was only for three hours; she woke at first light and was unable to go back off.

Now she was up and it was daylight she felt more comfortable. Switching on the TV and selecting a music channel she got herself a coffee, cereal and grapefruit for breakfast and in between mouthfuls sang along to Rihanna. After washing the pots she bummed around until 11 a.m., sorting out her wardrobes and cleaning the bathroom – something she hadn't got around to yesterday – and then got ready to meet Alex. They were meeting at Gaucho's, the riverside restaurant by Richmond Bridge. They had been there before. It was an expensive but always enticing menu, wonderfully cooked and prepared food and the setting was gorgeous. Just the thought of meeting Alex had set her heart fluttering and taken her mind off James Green.

Scarlett stepped out of the shower and wrapped a towel around her before gazing into the mirror. She was shocked by her appearance – her face was pale and drawn. She pinched her cheeks to put a little colour in them; she would need an extra dollop of make up today, she told herself as she made her way into the bedroom. Three-quarters of an hour later, moisturised and face painted, she pulled on her new buys, added a leather jacket and a pair of heels she'd not worn for a while, checked her appearance in the mirror and left the house. The restaurant was under three-quarters of a mile away, and although the sky was overcast it wasn't cold, so she decided to take a steady walk along the towpath.

Alex was waiting for her outside the restaurant. He greeted her with a gentle embrace and kiss to the cheek which she reciprocated. He was wearing the eau-de-cologne she'd bought him for Christmas and she lingered a little longer, taking in the smell, her heart bolting for a moment before she caught herself and drew away.

Eyeing her up and down, he said, 'You look lovely.'

'Thank you. I see you've made an effort yourself,' she responded.

He gave a short laugh. 'You don't change Scarlett. Fancy a beer before we eat? I've booked a table'

She did. She nodded.

They entered the restaurant and Alex checked in with the maitre de, informing him they wanted a drink before taking their table. They made their way to the bar and Alex ordered two beers in bottles, wedges of lime jammed into the necks.

After chinking bottles in salute, Scarlett took a sip on her beer. The tangy lager instantly refreshed her dry throat. She savoured the coldness of the liquid travelling into her stomach and for the first time that week she felt herself unwinding.

'This brings back memories,' said Alex.

Scarlett met Alex's gaze. His wide smile was showcasing a beautiful set of teeth. She felt her face flush. 'Good memories.'

Holding onto her look he said, 'So what you been up to? Has your week picked up since the court case? Have you got over what happened to your witness?'

She offered up a wan smile. 'A little, but I can't help but think how sad Claudette must have been to have done that and whether I'm to blame. I've asked myself a few times whether I was so caught up in getting Green convicted that I ignored her feelings.'

He grabbed her hand. 'Don't think that for one minute. I know you, Scarlett. One thing you are good at is supporting and helping people. That girl taking her own life wasn't your fault. You weren't to know what was going on inside her head. You did what you thought was best.'

'I know deep down I did my best, but what happened made me look at myself. I have to admit that, selfishly, my initial feeling when I found her was that a rapist was going to go free.'

'That's just a natural reaction. You'd put so much effort into capturing him. I'm sure if he strikes again you'll be there to feel his collar.'

'I'll bloody make sure I am.'

Squeezing her hand and then releasing it he said with a mischievous smile, 'And when you do, give him a swift kick in the balls on behalf of all his victims.'

His gallows humour lifted her. She wanted to tell him about what had happened yesterday but his throwaway comment was a prompt for her to keep the atmosphere light so she responded with, 'I certainly will. And I'll make sure I'm wearing my motorcycle boots.'

They let out a laugh together causing a few heads at nearby tables to turn.

Alex leaned in and said softly, 'I think we're lowering the tone. Come on let's have another drink and then we'll sit down and order.'

The hour and a half they were at their table flew by. The food as usual was wonderful and the conversation flowed as well as the bottle of wine they ordered. They even flirted with one another. Afterwards Alex paid the bill. She had tried to insist on splitting it but he said my treat – and wouldn't have it any other way.

As she rose Scarlett had to catch herself. She felt slightly tipsy. Alex gently grabbed hold of her arm. 'Come on we'll have a stroll and wear off some of this booze, then what you say we go over to my place and I make us a coffee? I've just bought this great espresso machine and I need to try it out.'

Scarlett met his sparkling blue eyes. 'That sounds lovely.'

Twenty-eight

Opening her eyes to the sight of heavy black drapes drawn across the window threw Scarlett into a state of confusion. Then she remembered where she was and started to relax; Alex's bedroom was a stark contrast to her own – mostly greys and blacks – very manly, though it was tasteful and nicely decorated. She turned over with a smile. Alex had his back to her and she lay for a moment listening to his gentle snuffle, running her eyes along the contours of his well-defined shoulder and neck muscles. Her smile stretched further. Images of yesterday tumbled inside her head. They hadn't had coffee when they got back to his place, instead Alex had opened another bottle of wine and they had drunk that. Then they'd had sex. It was spontaneous, passionate and hurried; they had pulled and tugged at each other's clothes lustfully, and spilled to the floor in the lounge, thrashing and grabbing at one another and climaxing together in minutes. Short though it was, it had left them both breathless and exhausted. They had stared up at the ceiling, holding hands and laughed about who had made the first move. 'It was you,' Alex had quipped. 'You couldn't resist me.' She had nudged him playfully, but knew he was right – she had. After they had got their breath back, they had showered together, tenderly soaping one another as if touching each other was a new experience. It had aroused them both again and Alex had carried her to his bedroom where the sex had been longer, slower and more intimate. When he had asked her to stay the night it had been such an easy decision for her to say yes.

Glancing over Alex's head she sought out the bedside clock. The green digits told her it was 7.18 a.m. Her head shot up. 'Shit!'

Beside her Alex jumped, 'What?'

Scarlett was swinging her legs out of bed. 'I'm going to be late for work.' She skipped to the bathroom – she needed the toilet. 'Bloody hell, I haven't got my clothes here or anything.' She called back, shutting the door.

Alex hauled himself out of bed and pulled on his pants. He sought out his shirt and trousers but they weren't anywhere to be seen. Then he remembered – they were still in the lounge among Scarlett's clothes from yesterday afternoon. As he went to find them he called, 'Grab a quick shower and I'll drive you over to your place to get changed. You shouldn't be too late.'

***

At the risk of getting a ticket Alex put his foot down to get Scarlett home, nevertheless she was still running late, and changed quickly. She decided to give styling her hair a miss and instead fashioned it up with grips. The same went for her make-up; as Alex drove she used the passenger visor mirror to repair her face. As the car came to a stop outside Sutton Police Station she took a last look in the mirror, and reasonably happy with her appearance, popped up the visor. It was just after 8.30 a.m.; half an hour late: She had already texted Tarn to cover for her. Reaching behind and snatching up her bag off the back seat she opened the door.

'Hey, where's my goodbye kiss?'

Scarlett turned to face Alex. His mouth was puckered in exaggerated fashion. She laughed and leaned in to plant a kiss on his lips. He grabbed the back of her neck, pulling her closer and began exploring her mouth with his tongue. She could feel the roughness of his unshaven stubble prickling her chin and felt herself being turned on. Right now though was not the time or place for these feelings, she told herself. She put a hand on his chest and slowly but forcibly pushed him back. 'Whoa tiger,' she said. 'I've got work to go to. I'm late enough as it is.' She opened the door. 'I'll ring you later,' and swinging out a leg she added, 'And thanks for the lift. I really appreciate it.'

'You're welcome.'

'Catch up at the weekend?' She explored his face, remembering the flux of their relationship and also recollecting it had been her idea to cool things between them. When Alex answered, 'Yeah that would be good,' she felt overwhelmed with joy. She blew him a kiss, closed the door, and with a spring in her step made her way into the station.

Twenty-nine

Still breathless from her run up the stairs, Scarlett walked into the Homicide Department doing her best to appear business-like, but as she let the door close behind her the sight of everyone seated around the conference table caused a moment of angst: Morning briefing was still in session. And, DI Taylor-Butler was taking it. *Fuck!*

Faces lifted her way and the DI's head turned. He said, 'DS Macey, so glad you can join us.' He pointedly looked at his watch.

'Fuck off prick,' Scarlett muttered beneath her breath so no one could hear. Then, putting on a flustered look, she moved to the table and said, 'I'm so sorry, crisis at home! The shower went on the blink. Couldn't get it to shut off. Thankfully a neighbour, who's a plumber, sorted it.' Alex had given her the excuse during their journey in. She'd told him she wouldn't need it, now she was grateful he had.

'All right DS Macey, don't bore us with the details. I'll expect you to make your time up.'

As she took up her seat she spotted Ella across the table. Her friend rolled her eyes and she gave a quick flick of her chin. The look said, 'ignore him.' Scarlett returned a half-smile and set her bag down on the floor.

DI Taylor-Butler continued with briefing and Scarlett realised they were discussing the aftermath of George and Ella's domestic murder; George's voice had an edge of frustration as he revealed the husband was on bail for an assault on his wife six weeks previously. The officers who had dealt with him had requested he be remanded, but magistrates had deemed him not to be a danger and released him on bail.

Sadly, Scarlett had heard this all too often.

The DI did a round-robin, confirming that there were no other enquiries pending, shut up his daily journal, and finished with, 'Okay everyone, so except for some mopping up to do with the takeaway stabbings across in Streatham the decks are clear, yes?' He watched several nodding heads. 'Right, good job everyone. Unless there's anything else to discuss I'll close briefing.'

Scarlett gave a sharp cough which attracted everyone's attention. Turning to the DI she said, 'I'd like to discuss James Green.'

Taylor-Butler's face hardened. 'What about James Green?'

'Now we haven't got anything on I'd like to target him.'

'Haven't we already discussed this?' There was a harsh note in his voice.

'We have, but he's stalking me.'

The DI's eyes narrowed. 'What do you mean stalking you?'

'He followed me to the supermarket on Saturday and stood outside waving at me. And I think he was outside Kerrie Tornese's flat the other day photographing me on his phone.' She didn't mention the hooded jogger she'd seen during her run: she hadn't seen the person's face.

'James Green was outside the supermarket waving at you?' His tone was mocking. 'And you think you saw him on the Winstanley Estate?'

'Yes.' She could feel her hackles rising. 'I'm sure it was him. He was in the crowd outside Kerrie Tornese's flat and he ducked when I spotted him.'

'You can definitely identify him?'

She thought a moment, 'Not definitely. No. It's a gut feeling.'

'A gut feeling!'

The DI pulled at the collar of his shirt, something she knew he always did when he was getting wound up. 'The fact that he was at the supermarket waving at me makes me think it was him.'

'But you can't be definite?' What about CCTV at the scene?'

'It looks out over the car park.'

'You have no concrete evidence it was him on the Winstanley Estate.' His cheeks reddened. 'So, based on evidence that he waved at you at the supermarket on Saturday, you say he's stalking you?'

'Look, I know its flimsy but…'

Taylor-Butler held up a hand, '…There's no but at all DS Macey. It is flimsy. Full stop. The fact that James Green happened to be outside a supermarket where you were shopping is not what I would define as stalking. And let's not lose sight of the fact that Professional Standards are still investigating the suicide of Claudette Jackson. I think given *that*, the last thing *we* want to be doing is targeting James Green at this time for something we cannot prove.' He pushed himself up from the table and picked up his journal. 'Unless James Green commits an offence, you will not go near him. And even then I will be assigning another team. Do I make myself clear?'

She didn't respond, but studied his face. He was beetroot.

'Do I make myself clear?'

Biting her tongue, she answered, 'Very clear.'

'Good. That is the last I want to hear on this matter.' With that, he stomped out.

After the DI left and the squad broke away from the conference table to return to their desks, Scarlett remained seated. Her chest was tight and inside she was seething. She was telling herself to stay calm, and without making it obvious she was taking deep breaths, fighting hard to keep it together and maintain a professional veneer. Finally, she glanced up to see Tarn looking her way. He didn't look his usual self; he was unshaven and his hair wasn't waxed. Seeing him like that broke across her thoughts. Picking up her bag, she headed to him, 'Thank you for covering for me at briefing. How did it go? I'm guessing you filled him in about Kerrie Tornese?'

Tarn nodded. 'Yeah, he said we'd done a good job.'

'Some praise then?'

He broke into a grin, 'You could say that.'

On a softer note she said, 'How did this weekend go with Trish? Dare I ask?'

The grin disappeared. 'Not good. In fact, bloody awful. It became one big rowing match in the end. I ended up walking out before I did something stupid. She texted me to tell me not to come back. I've slept in a B&B for the past two nights.'

'Oh gosh Tarn, I'm so sorry. Look you don't need to stay in a B&B, I've got a spare room at my place. Rose'll not mind, she only stays once in a blue moon anyway. You know what she's like - she prefers living in squats with her mates.'

'Thanks Scarlett, but I've spoken to mum and dad. They say I can have my old room back. It means a fair run into work, but I'm taking up the offer until I can get myself sorted. But I won't be able to pick you up for a while.'

'Don't worry about that. I've got the train and my bike. You just get yourself sorted, and if you need any time off just let me know.'

'Thanks, I will.' Turning he said, 'I'm just going for a coffee, want one?'

'Love one. I haven't had time for my fix yet this morning.'

She watched her partner as he headed for the door. He was walking like a wounded animal. She'd never seem him like this. She vowed to keep an eye on him.

As Tarn left the room she reached her desk, planted her bag down, slipped off her jacket and switched her gaze to other matters. Ella Bloom was on the phone, working her computer as she talked. Scarlett strolled across and Ella lifted her head. Scarlett expected her to be a vision of happiness but her face showed no emotion and as she sought out Ella's left hand she saw there was no ring on her finger. Suddenly, she felt awkward.

Ella finished her call and said, 'I see TB gave you a hard time again. I don't know how you put up with it Scarlett.'

She wanted to respond with, 'He resents me because I'm brighter than he is, and he's a sexist, bigoted, bullying prick.' Wanted to, but that wasn't her style. She would deal with him in her way, and in her own time, like she had done before; finding his DNA on bedding at a crime scene last year – a BDSM brothel – had been a coup, and she'd already hit him once with it: It was still in her armoury. Smiling inwardly she said, 'Oh well, you know what he's like. He'll grow up one day.' She gave a narrow smile. 'I'm sure James Green will come again and then I can always say " 'I told you so".' Taking a deep breath, she continued, 'Anyway, what about *you*?' She pointed to Ella's left hand, and leaning in and speaking in a near-whisper said, 'I was going to ask you how you got on this weekend. Ryan didn't propose then?'

Her poker-face broke, lighting up, 'Yes, he did.'

'But no ring?'

Ella nodded vigorously, and quickly looking around, put a finger to her lips and softly answered, 'I've taken it off. For now. Ryan's asked me not to wear it until next weekend. We're having a big get together with our families to make it official.' Indicating the detectives in the room she added, 'I'm keeping it low-key until next weekend, so keep it to yourself for now.'

Scarlett gave her two-thumbs up, and whispered, 'Congratulations Ella. That's wonderful.' Then, making a zipping motion across her mouth added, 'I promise I'll not say anything. I'm so happy for you.'

'Thank you. You only need to keep it quiet until Friday. I'm telling everyone then. I'm having a cocktails night in town. You've nothing on, have you?'

Scarlett so much wanted to tell her about Alex, but she still wasn't sure if there was anything permanent again about their relationship, and so instead she answered, 'Wouldn't miss it for the world. Its ages since I've had a cocktail night.'

Thirty

Guiltily, Scarlett removed the batch of folders and envelopes from her work bag and dropped them onto the kitchen work surface, letting out sigh. She had surreptitiously removed documents and photographs from folders relating to the James Green case, secreting them first into her desk drawer, and then, when she was sure no one was looking, hiding them away in her bag to bring home. She would have preferred not to be so secretive but DI Taylor-Butler's intransigence over Green had left her no option. She had told no one. Not even Tarn. If there were to be consequences for her actions then she had to take them alone.

For a moment she stared at the small stack. She didn't know what she was going to gain from gathering it but she couldn't just do nothing; James Green needed to be bought to account for what he'd done to those girls.

After making a coffee she changed out of her work clothes, slipped on joggers and a T-shirt and returned to the kitchen. She prepared a tuna salad, then picked up the folders, tucked them under an arm, and juggling them with her plate of food went through to the lounge and set them down on the coffee table. Bent forward on the sofa she picked at her salad with a fork while emptying out the contents of the folders and envelopes. Most of what she had brought home was what was referred to as 'unused material'; information which didn't help with the prosecution case and hadn't been submitted as evidence for court. There were statements from officers who had searched James Green's flat, detailing what had been recovered, together with CSI photographs of the interior of his house. It was the stuff she'd not really concentrated on when she'd put together the case file because it wasn't relevant to the prosecution. Now she wanted to go back through it all to see if she'd missed anything.

Pushing aside her empty plate, Scarlett fanned out the photos and began studying them in detail. For the best part of an hour she picked up each image individually, drifted her eyes over the picture, and then set it to one side and picked up another. CSI had photographed each room in Green's flat before it had been searched. In some cases, half a dozen shots had been taken of a room. They formed a good catalogue of his home life. As she finished looking at them, Scarlett leaned back against the sofa cushions. Something was off but she couldn't put her finger on it, so she decided to go through a couple of the searching officer's statements. Maybe one of those would trigger what was playing on her mind.

After the third statement, she stretched and closed her eyes, mentally reacquainting herself with James Green: He was twenty-six, had no known family and no girlfriend that they knew of, and lived alone in a flat in Twickenham. When she had checked him out, Scarlett was surprised he had not come to the attention of the police until his arrest four months ago. Difficult to believe, knowing what he'd done, and so she'd dug around beyond the Police Intelligence Unit, speaking to colleagues in probation and social services, but still there was nothing. She had even gone back in to the archives, looking for any unsolved sex crimes that matched his description. Nothing. And yet the nature and circumstances of the offences were not random: Last year over a three-month period he had attacked and raped a number of girls at knifepoint in the grounds of Richmond University, using the guise of a racing cyclist passing through – that had earned him the nickname of 'The Lycra Rapist'. When they had finally caught him and searched his place they had found nothing of evidential value. They'd found none of the cycle clothing that the witnesses and victims had described, although they learned he'd had a small bonfire in a rusted oil drum beneath the flats days before he'd been arrested, and neither had they found a mobile or personal computer that might have helped place or link him to the scene. It had been a frustrating result, and although Scarlett firmly believed Green's attacks had been targeted – that he had carefully selected his victims by stalking them first, as implied by Claudette Jackson when they had interviewed her – they had not been able to prove it.

Scarlett's eyes snapped open. *There has to be something in this lot that I've missed.* She picked up another couple of officer's statements. The first one only took five minutes to read and she skim-read the second. And, there she found it – second paragraph – an item the constable had recovered; a phone charger. *A phone charger, but no phone.* Her eyes were drawn back to the photographs. As she revisited the images of each of the rooms in James Green's flat things were falling into place, but she needed someone else's opinion to reinforce her beliefs.

***

Alex sat beside Scarlett on the sofa, studying the photographs spread out over the table.

'Thanks for coming over Alex, I really appreciate it. Have a look through these and tell me what you see.' Scarlett had already confessed to surreptitiously obtaining the photographs that day and explained her reason for doing so, and why they had been originally snapped by CSI officers during the search of James Green's home. She had phoned Alex because he'd viewed thousands of evidential photographs in his time as an officer in Military Intelligence, and although this was different, his skill for observation was what she needed right now.

He studied them for several minutes. 'You say these are all shots taken of the same flat?'

Scarlett nodded 'Yes.'

'Well the first thing I see is order.' He glanced sideways. 'Has this guy got OCD?'

'I can remember thinking how tidy the place was when I first saw it but I didn't conduct the search. I left that to a specialist search team.'

'Well this is the tidiest, neatest places I have ever seen that is lived in by a bloke. I'm reasonably tidy because of my army training but this guy is ultra-tidy to a state of obsession. Most guys I know leave their stuff all over the place.'

Alex's comment triggered the memory of the mess in the police car, left there by two male colleagues. She nodded.

'It's almost as if he knew you were coming and got someone to come in and spring-clean the place.' He smiled at his own joke as he picked up a couple of photos of the kitchen. 'Take these for instance. The kitchen is the most usual place in the house to find things left out, especially tea and sugar containers etcetera, or a few dirty pots to be left lying around. In these, there are none of those things. His worktops are immaculate.' He looked at Scarlett. 'Did you look inside the cupboards?'

She shook her head. 'As I say I didn't do the search. It was all done by a search team. But I would have thought they'd have made a comment if something didn't look right.'

'Okay.' He laid down the kitchen images and picked up a couple of the lounge. 'In these I see someone who looks as though they can just afford the basics. All we have here is a room containing a small sofa, an armchair, an old television and a small sideboard, plus a couple of cheap prints on the wall. It looks more like a scene from an amateur dramatic stage production. This lounge serves its purpose but it doesn't really look as though it's lived in.'

Scarlett slapped him on the shoulder. 'Bingo. You've said the magic words "not lived in".'

'But you told me these were the photos of James Green's house you searched?'

'They are. And that what's been niggling me. I sussed it just before I rang you. I read a statement where an officer had recovered a phone charger but no phone. And that's what triggered it. He wasn't carrying a phone and we never found one. We didn't find a personal computer either, which although not a rarity, I would expect to have done with someone of his intellect. And when I looked over these photos again what hit me in the face was how sterile his house looked. Nowhere on display are any personal items. Like you say, it looked like something you'd expect to see in an amateur stage production. Also, when I've gone back through the statements from the search team, very little personal property was recovered; a couple of sports shirts and a pair of trainers, but that's it.' She met Alex's eyes. 'Tell me if I'm way off mark here, but what I think is that this may be a place where James Green gets his head down from time to time, but this isn't where he actually lives.'

Thirty-one

Ella Bloom's engagement party was at the So Bar, not far from The Green. It was a trendy place with white leather seating and atmospheric lighting and it served great cocktails.

Togged up in a backless short dress to show off her expensive spray-tan, and wearing heels for a change, Scarlett entered the heaving, noisy, bar, and threaded her way through a throng of overly loud revellers, seeking out Ella. It didn't take long to clock her. She was among a group of friends by the bar, swaying gently to the music. A petite size 10, with boyish hips, Ella was sporting a black clinging mini dress with black and gold heel ankle boots. The joyful smile she was casting around said everything about her mood.

Scarlett joined them and Ella greeted her with a cheek-kiss.

'Great you could come,' she said, talking above the music. 'I think you know everyone.'

Scarlett glanced around the group. She did. Most of them were cops. Three that weren't, she had met before on previous nights out. She acknowledged them all with a nod and a hi, and then pointing to the pink cocktails they were all holding she said, 'What's that you're drinking?'

Ella held up her half-empty glass, 'Don't know but it's lovely. We told the barman it was my engagement do and he made us this special cocktail. Try it.'

As she held out the glass for her to take a sip Scarlett spotted Ella's ring. It was a large square diamond set in white gold. She took hold of Ella's finger and eyed it closely. It dazzled under the lights. *It must have cost Ryan a packet.* 'That's gorgeous,' she said letting go of Ella's hand.

'It is, isn't it? Ryan's mum helped choose it. I love it.'

Scarlett tried Ella's cocktail. A strong taste of raspberry hit the back of her throat which was refreshing, and then came the after-kick of what she thought was vodka. 'Gosh that's strong. Bad head tomorrow,' she laughed. Catching the barman's attention, she ordered the same.

As all seats and tables had been taken, the group hugged one end of the bar, ordering more cocktails, chinking glasses, toasting Ella's engagement. Scarlett caught up with a couple of the crew from her early uniform days; she hadn't seen them since their last big get-together six months ago. Everyone was in high spirits. They gossiped, mainly about men. One of the girls had a new neighbour. 'He's really hot,' she told the group, 'A fitness instructor – I've asked for some personal training.' They howled with laughter and continued the wicked gossip. Then, half an hour in, a table became available and they made a bee-line for it, claiming it a split-second before another bunch of party-goers, laughing as they plonked themselves down.

Ella draped an arm around Scarlett's shoulder. She was with Michelle Finch, a detective sergeant from Brixton. Scarlett had met Michelle a few times and knew that she and Ella were very close, having joined together. Michelle had introduced Ella to Ryan.

'I was just telling Michelle about the shit you have to take from TB.' Ella was slurring.

Michelle said, 'You don't have to take it from him. Not in this day and age. I'd report him, the sexist twat. Get him moved.'

Michelle's gravelly voice always reminded her of Mariella Frostrup. Scarlett responded with a nervous laugh. She didn't want this conversation to develop – not when she was out for a night of enjoyment. 'Don't worry. He'll get his comeuppance. I'm saving something special for him.'

Michelle tapped her on the shoulder. 'Good on yer. And if you ever need back up, count me in.'

Nodding and smiling, Scarlett finished off her cocktail, and setting down her empty glass she said loudly above the din, 'Order me another Ella, I'm just going to the ladies.' She pushed herself up, went a little woozy and had to grab hold of the table to steady herself. 'Bloody hell Ella those cocktails are potent. Get me half of lager instead.'

'Lager!' exclaimed Ella. 'You've no chance. It's shots and Jagerbomb time.' Scarlett left an explosion of laughter behind as she tottered to the ladies on unsteady heels.

After using the toilet she took several sips of water, checked herself in the mirror, replenished her lipstick, flicked a few errant strands of hair back into place and then taking several deep breaths stepped out into the corridor. She was just checking that the hem of her dress had not ridden up when she became conscious of someone blocking her way. All she saw at first was a pair of Fred Perry trainers and a pair of jeans, and her breath caught as she clocked who they belonged to. James Green. His piercing blue eyes bored right into her with a look that was icy, almost threatening. She sobered up immediately.

'Hello Detective Macey. Fancy meeting you here.'

'What the fuck are you doing here?'

'Now that's not a very nice greeting for someone who's just having a quiet drink in town.'

'No you're fucking not! You're following me!'

'Now you're being paranoid. Can't a man have a drink in a bar?'

'Not the one I'm in.'

'That's not being friendly.'

'I'm not a friendly person towards someone like you.'

'What do you mean, someone like me?'

'Rapist.'

'Now, now, that was never proved was it? That kind of talk is slander.'

James Green's gaze trailed down her chest to below her waist. It was a slow and deliberate move and she could feel anger welling up inside. At the same time her stomach lurched and she felt sick. She launched herself at him, grabbing hold of his T-shirt and slamming him back against the wall. 'You fuck off out of my face now, or I'll fucking nick you.'

He looked stunned for a moment, then his expression altered, his pupils dilating so quickly that they were just beads of black. Staring. *Fucking Freaky.* And although she had him pinned against the wall the change unnerved her.

Knocking aside her hand, he straightened his T-shirt, locked eyes for a second and strolled away. 'You've not heard the last of me Detective Macey,' he called back as he made for the exit.

As Scarlett watched him leave she started to shake. 'The gloves are off James Green. I'm bringing you down,' she growled to herself. Then, trying her best to pull herself together, she headed back to the celebration.

Thirty-two

Scarlett spent most of the weekend recovering from the mother of all hangovers. She wrote Saturday off, lying on the sofa, feeling as if she was dying. On Sunday, she awoke feeling a little better, but still not back to her best, so she decided to go for a spin on her beloved Bonnie to blow away the cobwebs. She'd helped to restore the 1967 Triumph Bonneville T120 motorcycle with her dad when she was sixteen; he had brought it home as a wreck, and together they'd rebuilt it. He had taken her out on pillion for its first run and then taught her how to ride it. It became hers following his untimely death.

Scarlett only planned to take a short journey, but the urge to open up the bike for an adrenalin rush was too great and she ended up blasting down to Brighton and back. It did the trick in clearing her woolly head.

Sunday evening, still furious with James Green for hijacking her Friday night, she wrote in her work journal a summary of what had happened in the So Bar, determined to tackle it the next day. Once she told DI Taylor-Butler about Green's threat, he would have to back her up.

She planned to spend the remainder of her evening relaxing in front of the TV, catching up with a couple of programmes she had recorded, but after struggling through an episode of EastEnders, she turned it off, unable to get Green out of her mind. Sometimes Scarlett wished she could switch off her brain. The notion that he had another bolt-hole was bugging her and the only way it was going to go away was if she dealt with it there and then. So, booting up her laptop, she tested her theory by surfing the net. First port of call was Facebook, where she found seven James Greens in London, but none of the profile photos matched. Next, she Googled his name for an address check. There were 200 James Greens listed in the UK, with phone numbers, just 39 when the field was narrowed down to the London area. Many had middle names, which she hadn't given any thought to before and it made her realise this task was not going to be easy. As Scarlett hopped from one record to the next, a niggling doubt appeared – was James Green his real name? The DNA and fingerprints Green had given upon his arrest had been checked against the national database but there hadn't been a match. All that meant was that he hadn't been in custody before and wasn't wanted for any criminal matter. It didn't prove who he was.

Am I taking this too far?

With an exasperated sigh, Scarlett closed down her laptop and returned to the statements she'd borrowed from Green's case file. As she doubled back through them, and married them against the recovered exhibits, she realised that the only thing they had to confirm his identity was a driving licence and a couple of household bills. The household bills proved zilch and she knew how easy it was to get hold of a forged driving licence. They hadn't recovered any credit or debit cards, and when they had arrested him and brought him into custody, all he had on him was a little cash. This was going to require a lot more investigation, she thought as she bundled together the paperwork.

As Scarlett tucked the documents and photographs into her work bag, the sight of her mobile on the coffee table reminded her that she hadn't yet rang Ella to thank her for Friday night, and tell her about her confrontation with James Green; she hadn't mentioned it at the time because she hadn't wanted to put a dampener on the evening's fun. The call went to voicemail, and so texted her friend to thank her and tell her she'd been rough all through Saturday. She decided not to text anything about James Green, instead, she would tell Ella when she saw her at work.

Ella texted her back within a minute, 'Can't speak out with Ryan's family. Thanks I had a great time as well but the night was spoiled. We were broken into while we were out.'

Scarlett was taken aback. 'OMG. So sorry to hear that. Much damage. Was anything taken.'

'No thank God. Looks as if they were disturbed. Tell you about it tomorrow.'

For a moment Scarlett stared at her phone. James Green took solid form in her thoughts again. Was she stretching her imagination a little too far? It seemed too much of a coincidence that hours after bracing him up and he'd made his threat, Ella and Ryan's flat had been burgled.

Thirty-three

On Monday morning, Scarlett awoke refreshed and fired up for the week ahead. The decks were clear at work and she was going to air Friday night's episode involving Green and demand that something be done. It was going to wind up DI Taylor-Butler, but he could go take a running jump – he had dismissed her theory about her being stalked too easily and this second episode was more than enough proof. This time he hadn't a leg to stand on.

Checking that the papers from Green's case file were out of sight in her bag she set her house alarm, slammed the front door, rattling the handle to test it was locked, tucked her mane of red hair inside her helmet and mounted her motorcycle. Bonnie stuttered for a few seconds before erupting into a throaty roar as she throttled up. Then she rolled it out of her gate and onto the road and set off to the station. Unlike the previous day, she took a more leisurely ride into the office.

In the ladies, Scarlett peeled off her biking leathers, replaced her motorcycle boots with flat shoes and shook out her hair, running her fingers through it to remove the knots. Checking herself in the mirror, she did her best to palm out the creases in her slacks. Then, happy with her image, added a spot of lipstick and stepped out into the corridor.

As she entered the office, Scarlett held her bag close to her side, keeping the top firmly shut to hide Green's case notes as she headed to her desk. The office was back to normal. Members of both syndicates were in and the place was full of its customary early morning chatter: George Martin was perched on the edge of Carl Jenkins' desk being bullish with him and DC Shaun

Fletcher. From a couple of the raucous comments she gathered the conversation was about football; George was a Gunner and the other two were Hammers fans. Beyond them, at Rachel Cooper's desk, Ella was showing off her engagement ring; Rachel hadn't been able to make the celebrations because of a family commitment. Scarlett was about to head over to ask Ella about her burglary when Tarn cut across her line of sight, heading back to his desk with a brew. He smiled as he set down his mug but it wasn't his usual grin. It didn't light up his face like it usually did. In fact, she thought he looked washed out. There were rings around his eyes and his shoulders sagged. Scarlett changed her mind about going to see Ella. As Tarn dropped down into his seat she leaned over and said softly, 'Are you okay?'

He nodded back, but his face wasn't convincing.

'You don't look it, Tarn.'

'I'm fine, Scarlett.'

There was a sharp edge to his reply. 'Tarn, I can read you like a book. We need to talk. As soon as morning briefing's over you and I are going for a run out. I'm not taking no for an answer.'

Tight-lipped he mouthed, 'Yeah okay,' and then took a sip of his coffee.

'Good. I'm just going across to have a word with Ella. Get me a coffee will you?' Scarlett unlocked her drawers, placed her bag in the bottom one and was about to head across and speak to Ella when she spied a brown paper bag in her top tray. She studied it a second. It was sealed and labelled to Detective Macey. She said to Tarn, 'What's this?'

He shrugged. 'It was sitting there when I came in. It's probably from one of your many admirers.' His face became mischievous, 'TB, maybe.'

'Yeah sure.' Scarlett broke the seal and looked inside. Screwing up her face she said, 'Fruit.'

'Fruit?'

She tore one side of the bag and a couple of oranges tumbled onto her desk. 'When I say fruit – lemons and oranges.' She picked out a lemon and showed him.

'Just lemons and oranges?'

She nodded.

'That's a strange combination. Oh well at least it's a thought. Is there a note?'

She fished around among the fruit, but came out empty handed. 'Nope. No note.'

'Someone's thinking of you that's the main thing.'

She rolled across one of the oranges to Tarn and started to peel another. 'Well never say I don't share anything with you.'

Suddenly the office door crashed open and in strode DI Taylor-Butler.

Tarn hissed quietly, 'Oh, oh, your favourite person Scarlett, and he doesn't look too happy.'

'DS Macey,' the Detective Inspector called from the doorway.

Scarlett half-turned. His eyes were narrowed. If looks could kill, she thought.

'My office now!'

'What?'

'You heard.' With that he turned and left, crashing the door behind him.

All eyes were on Scarlett. Questioning. She shrugged her shoulders, threw up her hands in a 'no idea' gesture and made for the door. In the corridor, a twang of nerves caught her. Her stomach tightened. She wondered if he'd discovered the statements and photographs missing from the Green files. They were still in her bag in her bottom drawer. She mentally prepared an answer that wasn't far from the truth.

Taylor-Butler was already behind his desk when she entered his office. As usual there was no seat on offer so she stood before him.

He met her inquiring gaze, 'What the hell happened Friday night?'

For a second the question threw her. His face was red and looked about to burst. 'With regards?'

'James Green of course. Are you trying to be clever, or did you assault someone else while you were drunk?'

Her jaw dropped, flabbergasted he was talking to her in this manner, but she quickly recovered. 'Me? Assault James Green?'

'Are you saying you did not throw him against the wall and threaten him?'

She ran his question quickly around inside her head and answered, 'I can't believe I'm hearing this. Yes, I threatened to nick him, but that was because he was stalking me. I've already told you about the incident at the supermarket. I was out in Richmond with some friends, including Ella Bloom, on Friday night. We were in a bar and Green confronted me as I came out of the toilets.'

'Confronted you?'

'Yes, confronted me. So I challenged him and told him if he didn't get out of my face I was going to nick him. I've put it all in my journal. I was going to raise it at morning briefing. I want him warning for harassment.'

The DI gave a dismissive half-laugh. 'You want him warning for harassment?'

'Yes. This is the second time now.'

'His story is completely different.'

'His story?' Scarlett looked puzzled.

Taylor-Butler picked up some papers and shook them in her face. 'This is James Green's official complaint. He came in to see the Duty Inspector Sunday morning, alleging that he was drinking in town on Friday evening, he walked into the So Bar and you grabbed him by the T-shirt, threw him against the wall, banging his head, and then you started verbally abusing him and threatening him for no reason.'

'Oh come on, you are kidding me. You believe that?'

'Well it certainly looks like that from what I've seen.'

'What do you mean?'

'The Inspector didn't just take his word before formalising his complaint. He went to the bar and recovered the CCTV footage of the incident. I've seen it this morning and it doesn't make for pleasant viewing. It quite clearly supports his allegation.'

'I don't believe this.'

'The camera doesn't lie DS Macey.'

'No, I don't suppose it does, depending how you want to interpret it.'

'How do you mean how I interpret it? I don't interpret it any way other than how I see it. The CCTV clearly shows you pinning him against the wall by his T-shirt and you look as if you're threatening him. There is no evidence on the footage I've seen that shows he confronted you in a threatening manner in any way, shape or form.'

'Well I'm telling you he's stalking me. That was the second time he's shown up where I've been, and I also think he was at the incident on the Winstanley Estate, I've told you that. I want him warning for harassment.'

'And that is going to look really good, isn't it? Someone making a formal complaint against a police officer for assault is themselves warned for harassment.'

Scarlett was getting more and more wound up and doing her best to suppress her anger. Taking a deep breath, she said, 'So what you're saying is you're taking the word of a scrote against mine and doing nothing about it.'

The DI's face was almost blood red now. Through gritted teeth he steadily answered, 'What I'm saying, DS Macey, is that a formal complaint has been made against you for assault, and until that is investigated then nothing is being done about James Green. You can make your statement about what happened on Friday, but that is all. I want you going nowhere near him for now, and that is an order.' He gave her a long look, then, dropping the pages of James Green's statement on his desk, he locked together his fingers and said calmly, 'Can I give you some advice DS Macey? In a couple of days' time you will be interviewed by Professional Standards, I suggest you keep your head down until then and also smarten yourself up. We've had this conversation before about the amount of make-up you wear. This is not a fashion department. I want my detectives to look like detectives. This morning it looks as if you've crayoned your face on. I suggest that in future you come to work looking more presentable.'

Scarlett wanted to explode, but knew that was not going to get her anywhere. Turning sharply, she tramped out of the room and into the corridor, giving him the finger once out of view.

Thirty-four

Scarlett was taking shelter in the doorway of the coffee house, clutching two cappuccinos, looking out across the car park and debating what to do. It was bucketing down – slashes of rain were pinging off the tarmac like bullets. In the short time she had been inside, waiting for her order, the heavens had opened. She cursed when she saw how far away she had parked the car; she had chosen the back of the car park deliberately so that she and Tarn could talk but still have a full view of what was going on around them: That was what cops did.

Seeing no break in the slate coloured sky she made up her mind, took a deep breath and put in a dash. It was only forty yards to the car but by the time she reached it she was drenched.

Leaping inside she slammed the door shut and shuddered. 'Jesus,' she said, shaking her head, 'Where did that come from?' A spray of water from her hair spattered the windscreen, side window and Tarn.

He cursed.

She handed over Tarn's coffee before putting the key in the ignition and flicking on the wipers. They swished into overdrive, but the rain was hitting the windscreen with such force that they weren't having much effect and so after a few seconds she turned them off. 'Christ, I'm glad I'm not out in this.'

Tarn took the lid off his coffee and blew into it. 'It'll ease off soon.' He took a sip, lifting off the froth from the top. Wiping his top lip, he said, 'You know, you don't have to take that shit from TB, Scarlett. You should report him. He would if it was the other way round.'

'And where will that get me? You know what this job's like. They'll probably move me and I love working with this squad. It's all I've wanted to do since I joined the job.'

There was a moment's silence and then Tarn said, 'So you're backing off Green?'

'That's what he ordered.'

'That wasn't an answer, Scarlett.'

She met her partner's gaze and gave a wry smile. 'You bet your sweet life I'm not.' She continued, 'I was all geared up to go for the jugular this morning but Green has completely turned the tables on me. He's smart, you know. The CCTV will make it look as though I attacked him for no reason. He set me up. I'm going to have to back off for a while, but I've got something up my sleeve once things have died down.' She took a drink of her cappuccino and looked out at the rain pelting the windscreen. The inside was starting to mist up. 'Anyway, enough about my troubles, I want to know how you're going on.'

Tarn sighed heavily. 'Not good really. Things are starting to get to me. I never thought I'd feel like this. It's killing me not being able to see the kids! It's killing me, not seeing Trish! Sure, I'm really grateful to mum and dad for letting me move back – it's saved me a small fortune in hotel bills – but it's not like my own home. It feels so awkward. I mean it's a good six years since I left. I can see they've made a different life for themselves now. I'm just in the way.'

'I'm sure they're not thinking that.'

'I know they're worried about me, but at the same time I'm sure they wouldn't want me back full time.' Heaving another sigh, he said, 'This is that head's fault.'

'Do you definitely know it's the head she's seeing?'

'I don't have any proof, if that's what you mean, but I'm sure it is.' There was a silence and then he said, 'Do you know, right now, I could wring her fucking neck, and punch his fucking lights out.' With a sigh he added, 'But that's not going to get me anywhere is it?'

'It might make you feel better,' Scarlett half laughed. 'That's a bit like what I feel right now towards James Green and the DI.'

'Yeah I guess so. But then it might also mean we get arrested.'

'Ha, there is that to it.' Pausing a few seconds, she added, 'What we need is a cunning plan.'

They both burst out laughing.

Scarlett said, 'Look there's still the offer of crashing down at my place if it gets too much for you at your mum and dad's.'

'Thanks, I really appreciate that and I'll bear that in mind. I'm going to nip back home tonight. The kids normally go to Trish's mum and dad's today so I'm going to see if I can catch her and try and sort something out.'

Scarlett turned to him again, 'Would you have her back if she admitted it?'

Tarn didn't immediately respond, then said, 'I love her Scarlett.'

She could tell he was hurting inside and Scarlett decided it would be best to leave it there. She started the car and the wipers cleared the screen. She said, 'It's starting to ease off. We'll finish our coffee and head back in. I want to have a word with Ella before she leaves.'

***

Scarlett's jacket was still damp when she got back to the office. She took it off, gave it a shake and hung it over her chair. Ella was working at her desk and Scarlett was about to go across to have a word when she spotted the envelope, bearing the name, 'Detective Macey'. James Green leapt into her thoughts again: That's what he had called her on Friday when he had confronted her coming out of the toilets. With finger and thumb she gingerly picked it up by one corner and turned it over. On the back was penned 'You owe me x 5'. She read it again. It didn't mean a thing. The envelope looked to be empty yet she could feel by its weight that something was inside. Holding it up to the light she saw a round shape tucked in one corner. It looked like a small coin. Even more perplexed, she unpicked the seal and turned the envelope upside down. A dirty copper-coloured coin fell out. Judging by the young Queen Elizabeth's head on it, it was old. She picked the coin up and turned it over. It was a 1947 Farthing, long out of circulation. She double-checked inside the envelope to see if there was anything else. Nothing. Shaking her head, none the wiser, she pondered a moment, switching her attention between the coin she was holding and the envelope. It didn't have a stamp, which meant that someone must have left it at reception. She dialled the front desk number and it was picked up on the third ring. A familiar voice answered. 'Jenny, an envelope's been put on my desk. It actually says it's for Detective Macey. Did you put it there?'

The receptionist said, 'Yes I did Scarlett. You're the only person I know in this station with that surname. Why? Isn't it for you?'

'To be honest Jenny I don't know. The only thing inside it is an old coin. It doesn't make sense. Do you know who left it?'

'An old lady gave it to me. I didn't get her name. She just said it was for Detective Macey. I asked for her name, but she said it wasn't anything to do with her. She said she'd been asked to leave it for you. I assumed it was something you were expecting. Is something the matter?'

'No Jenny. I'm just puzzled by it that's all. It doesn't mean anything to me. Not to worry,' Scarlett hung up. After studying the envelope again, she shrugged, put the farthing back inside and shoved it into her top drawer. Across the room, Ella was still at her desk working at her computer. She mooched over.

Ella stopped typing and looked up. 'Oh hi, Scarlett. You okay?'

'I just wanted to ask you about your burglary. It must have ruined your night and your weekend?'

'It certainly put a dampener on things. I was glad Ryan was with me when we walked in. It really shook me up. You never think about how it affects anyone until it happens to you.'

'But thankfully they didn't take anything?'

'No not a thing. We're so fortunate. We can only think they must have been disturbed. I mean my work phone was in the kitchen on charge and my iPad was on the sofa. They're the first things you'd expect to get nicked.'

'All your jewellery left alone? And cash?'

She nodded. 'Nothing taken at all. They didn't even trash the place. If it hadn't been for the flat door being forced we'd have never have known anyone had broken in. The landlord's been good as gold. He came round on Saturday afternoon and put new locks on. Ryan and I made our own enquiries with our neighbours but none of them heard or saw anything. We can't even see how they got into the block. The main door downstairs hadn't been forced.'

'Did SOCO find anything?'

Tight-lipped she shook her head. 'Wearing gloves. They think a screwdriver, or something similar, was used on the lock. No, we've got away with it. You could say we were one of the lucky ones. This time. I tell you what though, it's made Ryan and me determined to get our own place now. You know what it's like once you've been targeted – always that chance they'll come back now they know how easy it is.'

Scarlett agreed with a nod. She had intended airing her thoughts about James Green, given what had gone on at Ella's engagement, but the fact that only she had been the brunt of his complaint, and no damage had been caused at Ella's place she decided that she'd got it wrong and kept her thoughts to herself. However, as she returned to her desk, she was still determined she was going to make his life a misery.

Thirty-five

Across from his home, Tarn sat in his car, eyes fixed on his front door. He had just turned off the engine and it ticked as it cooled and died. *A bit like my heart at the moment.* Taking a deep breath, he anxiously smoothed his sweaty hands around the steering wheel. His thoughts were in overdrive as he re-ran in his head what he wanted to say to Trish. He had thought of nothing else since he had set off from his parent's home three-quarters of an hour ago – the journey had been a blur – he'd been on auto-pilot all the way here. It wasn't just what he wanted to say but how he wanted to say it. That was important because he was hurting. Hurting because he wasn't the one in the wrong here: He had never been unfaithful, unlike some of his colleagues. He had always thought of their marriage as being rock solid: That Trish loved him as much as he loved her. *Just shows you how wrong I've been.* He smacked the steering wheel. It hurt his hand. He loved her, but he also hated her for she had done. As he removed the key from the ignition he told himself that getting angry was not going to resolve things today. He took a deep breath before leaving his car. *Get your shit together Tarn.*

He sauntered across the road and entered his front garden. Tapping gently on the front door he opened it cautiously and stepped into the hall, calling out 'Hi.'

Trish appeared in the kitchen doorway at the end of the hall, wiping her hands. Her surprised look quickly turned sheepish. 'Oh, I wasn't expecting you.'

Trish retreated back into the kitchen and Tarn followed. She was tidying away the pots.

'Heather and Dale are next door playing with Lucy and James. Do you want me to go and get them?' she said, putting three plates into the cupboard.

'It's you I've come to see, Trish.' He took a step nearer and she turned to face him. He caught a whiff of her perfume. Fresh flowers. It was the one he'd bought her at Christmas.

'I don't want a row, Tarn.'

'I don't want to row, Trish. I just want to sort things out.'

'Sort what things out?'

'We need to talk.'

'There's nothing to talk about.'

'Look Trish, I know you've been seeing someone. I just want to sit down and talk things through.'

She leaned back against the work surface. 'I've already told you I'm not seeing anyone. You're being ridiculous. When do I have time to see anyone?'

'All those times you've told me you've been working late, and that teacher's conference you told me you were at that weekend. I'm not stupid.'

Trish laughed sharply, 'You're being paranoid.'

'I am not being paranoid. You've been seen in the pub with him.'

'We've already had this discussion. That was once, and it was after we'd all been working late because of the Ofsted visit.'

Tarn could feel himself getting agitated. He breathed deeply, locking eyes with her.

She looked away.

'Trish, I can tell you're lying. I know it's Adam Witton.'

'This is ridiculous. He's my boss. We work closely together that's all.'

He sniped back, 'I wonder if his wife thinks it's ridiculous.'

Trish pushed herself away from the work surface. 'Don't you dare!'

'Do you know Trish, I can't believe this of you. All this time together. Haven't I always been there for you?'

'Well that's a debateable statement.' She put her hands on her hips.

'What's that supposed to mean?'

'You saying you've always been there for me. You're always at work. I might as well be single.'

'Oh come on Trish. I work long hours because that's my job. That's what detectives do. You know that. Anyway, it's that extra money that pays for this house. Without it we'd still be in a pokey little flat.'

She stared blankly for a few seconds, then said, 'At least I was happy back then.'

Her response tore through him. 'What the fuck is that supposed to mean? Aren't you happy now? Don't I make you happy any more?'

'If you want to know the truth, then, no! I haven't been happy for ages. And if you'd have been at home more regular you'd have seen that.'

Tarn bit his bottom lip and clenched his fists. 'That is so unfair Trish. We need my extra money for this house.' He drew in a breath but couldn't control himself any longer. He said loudly, 'I suppose you're going to say that blue-eyed, fucking super head, Adam Witton, makes you happy?'

'If you want a truthful answer, then, yes. He's everything you're not.'

Tarn pulled back his fist.

***

In his parked car, a few doors down from his parents' house, Tarn rested his head against the driver's window and eyed the red, sore knuckles of his right hand. They had already started to swell and he squeezed his hand into a ball. The pain made him wince. He hadn't intended losing his temper but those last words of hers had stung like barbed wire and he'd lashed out. Now he was regretting it. The sudden rap on his window made him jump. A uniformed officer was peering in and indicating for him to open his window. He powered it down.

'Is it DC Scarr?' the officer asked.

He pulled his hand out of view, 'Yes.'

'Would you mind stepping out of the car please?'

Thirty-six

Scarlett was getting ready for bed – in the middle of brushing her teeth – when she heard her work phone ringing from the bedroom. She switched off the electric toothbrush, spat out a mouthful of toothpaste and dashed to the next room, snatching up the phone from her bedside table. It was DCI Diane Harris – head of the squad. Startled to be receiving this call she answered, 'Good evening boss. This is a surprise. I thought you were still on holiday until tomorrow.'

'I am officially, but something's cropped up that needed my attention.'

Scarlett's stomach flipped. *James Green's complaint. Shit!* Hesitantly, she replied, 'Oh yes, anything serious?'

'About as serious as they could be! Listen, have you spoken to Tarn recently?'

'Tarn?' The DCI's question had thrown her.

'Yes Tarn. When did you last see him or speak with him?'

'This afternoon, as we finished work. Why? Is something the matter?'

'What was he like? What did he say to you?'

This was not what she was expecting. *What the fuck's going on?* Stumbling over her words she answered, 'He was okay, why? I don't know what you mean about what did he say? He was just normal. We talked about work.'

'Do you know if he's been having problems at home? Has he said anything to you about his wife, Trish?'

Scarlett wondered where this was going. Had Tarn done something stupid? Cautiously she said, 'I believe they've been going through a bad patch recently.'

'And you've not been in contact with him since you finished work?'

'No boss, no. Has something happened?'

There was a moment's silence before Diane Harris said, 'Tarn's under arrest, Scarlett.'

'Under arrest?'

'I want you to join me at his house.'

'You mean at Brentford?'

'Yes, I'll fill you in when you get here.'

***

Scarlett had to brake sharply as she turned into the street where her partner lived. Twenty yards away a patrol car was in the middle of the road, sideways on, its top lights flashing, washing the surroundings in weak tones of blue. Behind it, crime scene tape was drawn across the street, sealing it off. More police vehicles and an ambulance were lined up either side. *What the fuck?* This was serious. She coasted towards the pavement edge, killed the engine and pulled her bike onto its stand. Taking off her helmet, she placed it on the seat, unclipped the back box, lifted out her forensic suit and draped it over her arm as she made her way to police car blocking the road. As she got close, the driver's door opened and a female PC climbed out.

Scarlett unzipped her leather suit to pull out the lanyard holding her warrant card and flashed it. 'DS Macey,' she announced. 'I'm looking for DCI Harris.'

The young officer quickly eyed her identification. 'She's in the detective's house. CSI have just got here.'

Not wishing to appear as if she didn't know what was happening, and too scared to ask the obvious – is it a murder – Scarlett headed for the first cordon, ducked beneath the tape, stepped into her all-in-one forensic suit and hurried to Tarn's house, a three-bedroom, red-brick semi on a corner plot. She had been here many times. Tonight, arc lights on tripods slashed through the darkness, lighting up its frontage. Two white suited members of the Forensic team were erecting a tent around the front door as she approached the gate. She was about to step onto the drive when a voice to her right stopped her in her tracks.

'Scarlett.'

She recognised DCI Diane Harris's voice, though she didn't recognise her in the Tyvek suit, with its hood up and face mask on.

Scarlett bundled up her hair. 'Hello boss,' she said coaxing her hair into the hood of her suit. 'Is this as bad as I think it is?'

The DCI pulled down her face mask. 'Tarn's wife's dead. We arrested him a couple of hours ago near his parents' home.'

Scarlett had expected to hear this, or something similar but the words still stunned her when they came. She felt a sudden stabbing to her chest and her stomach flipped. For a moment she stood there, unable to move. *Fuck me, he's killed her!*

'I'm sorry to call you out, Scarlett. I know you and Tarn are close, so you don't have to do this if you don't want to, but I need to know what's being going on between them.'

The DCI's voice brought her thoughts back to the present. Scarlett nodded slowly. 'No, I understand boss. I'm okay with this.'

'Okay, good. C'mon then I'll show you what we've got.' She pulled her face mask back on and with muffled voice added, 'Prepare yourself, it's not pretty in there.'

As they zipped open the forensic tent's entrance the first thing that hit Scarlett was the metallic aroma which assaulted her even before she stepped inside the house. It should have prepared her for the sight ahead but the carnage in the hallway stopped her in her tracks. For a moment she stood there, stunned. There was so much to take in. Blood and blood-spatter was everywhere. Floor, walls, even the ceiling. The wooden floor, especially, was swimming in it. Some was starting to congeal, but the majority was still fluid, crimson in colour and judging by the track marks it looked as though Trish had thrashed around before she had died. She lay at the end of the hallway, her body half inside the kitchen.

As if following her thoughts DCI Harris said, 'It looks as though she was initially stabbed by her attacker the moment she opened the front door and tried to escape but didn't get very far. There's not a part of her body that hasn't been stabbed. This was frenzied.' She held Scarlett back on the threshold 'I don't want you to go any further, forensics have not even started here yet. I just wanted you to see what's happened here. Now we need to talk.'

Thirty-seven

DCI Harris took morning briefing. She stood in front of the murder board, scanning the room, nodding occasionally as she engaged glances with members of her team. She looked business-like, her flaxen hair parted slightly off centre, resting on her shoulders, framing a serious looking face. She wore a silk blouse – the whiteness of which showed off a deep tan from her recent holiday – beneath a fitted light grey pinafore dress and low heel shoes. Her glowing complexion made her look younger than her 40 years. Stirring into action, she stuck up an A4 photograph of Trish Scarr, sitting at a table in a restaurant. She looked elegant, fair hair piled up and a string of pearls around her neck and she was holding up a glass of wine in salutary fashion and smiling broadly. Happier times. The photo was in stark contrast to the three crime scene images pinned up of her lying crumpled in congealed blood.

DCI Harris called the room to order, 'Okay everyone, heads up. At just after 7.30 p.m. last night, twenty-nine-year-old Trish Scarr's body was discovered in the hallway of her home by her immediate neighbour. She had been repeatedly stabbed. As we all know, Trish is the wife of Tarn.'

Some of the team exchanged sombre looks.

Diane Harris indicated the murder scene images. 'A post-mortem carried out in the early hours reveals she had been stabbed and slashed eighty-seven times by a single bladed knife approximately six inches in length. It more than probably is a kitchen knife. There is not a part of her body that has not been attacked. The majority of the stab wounds are to her upper chest, face and head, but she also has wounds to the tops of her legs and defence wounds to her hands and arms. The wound that killed her was to her throat but the pathologist told me that many of the wounds inflicted to her chest would have eventually killed her because of their severity.' Diane paused. 'This was a really vicious and frenzied attack. From the trail of blood and spatter on the walls it would appear the attack started close to the front door, carried on along the hallway and ended by the door leading into the kitchen where she finally collapsed. It would have gone on for several minutes.'

Diane spent a moment studying her team. Some looked shocked, and she guessed it wasn't only because of the brutality of it all, but because this was very close to home. 'As I said earlier, Trish was found like this by her immediate neighbour, Grace Appleby, at around 7.30. Dale and Heather, Trish and Tarn's two children, had been playing with Grace's two children, next door, and the arrangement was that Trish would collect them at 7 p.m., but Grace had heard an argument through the walls of her house at about 6.30, and saw Tarn storming away from the house about quarter-to-seven and driving away in his car. She knows that Trish and Tarn have recently split up, because Trish had told her, and so she decided to give her some time before she let the children go back. When Trish didn't come around she went next to door to check on her and found her as you see in the photos. She immediately called emergency services.'

Diane looked to the room again, seeing a mixture of emotions on faces. Scarlett's looked glum. From talking to her the previous night, she knew Scarlett was the only member of the squad aware of Tarn's and Trish's domestic upheaval. The news she had just delivered would have come as a surprise and a shock. 'I'm guessing you all know by now that Tarn has been arrested. At eight-thirty last night, following Grace Appleby's information, a call was put out for him to be detained and he was found sitting in his car a few doors down from his parents' home, where he has been staying for the past few days. This is where I came into it.' She continued, 'Tarn was taken to Western Homicide Command and interviewed under caution by Detectives from there. His clothing and vehicle have been seized and he is currently on bail and suspended.' She took a deep breath. 'I don't want anyone reading anything into this now. As you all know this is standard procedure, it matters not that he is one of our own.'

'Is there any evidence to suggest it is Tarn?' It was George Martin posing the question. His voice was low, as if almost too afraid to ask.

Diane shook her head. 'We don't have anything just yet. Far too early. The forensic team have recovered hair, fibre and prints from the hallway and they have found scrapings of flesh underneath Trish's fingernails where she's fought for her life. All that has been bagged and tagged. We should have a result in the next forty-eight hours. For now, we have Grace Appleby's statement about the argument she heard, and her sighting of Tarn leaving the house and driving away three-quarters of an hour before she found Trish's body. Some house-to-house was done last night, but that didn't add anything. We'll be following up that aspect today.'

'What about the weapon. A kitchen knife you say. Was it left at the scene?' Ella Bloom asking this one.

Diane again shook her head, 'We haven't yet found any knife that matches the one that inflicted Trish's injuries. Forensics have been working in the house throughout the night and a fresh team will be taking over this morning. Search officers will begin a search of the gardens and street later today. With regards forensics, you don't need me to tell you how difficult this is going to be. This is also Tarn's house, so traces of him will be everywhere, and he was seen there, and has admitted being there, less than one hour before her body was found.' She added, 'Once again I don't want you reading anything into that comment. Yes, Tarn is a suspect, but it's still too early in our investigation to suggest that he is our *only* suspect.'

Scarlett said, 'Has Tarn said anything?'

'I wasn't party to the interview but detectives who spoke with him tell me he was open with them, and the officer who initially arrested him has said he appeared genuinely shocked when told the reason for his arrest and his clothing shows no sign of having blood on it. He's told them he went to his house with the intention of sorting things out with Trish, but it deteriorated into a full-blown argument, during which he punched the wall in the kitchen out of frustration. Then he left. He has been examined and the knuckles of his right hand are swollen, and there is damage to the wall by the door between the kitchen and the hallway, which backs up that story. He's said that after leaving his home he drove to the Brewery Tap pub in Brentford, where he had two beers and then drove to his parent's home where he was detained. I have listed actions for visits to the Brewery Tap, and for CCTV and ANPR checks to be made along the route Tarn said he took.'

'What about the head at Trish's school – the man Tarn believes was having an affair with Trish?' asked Scarlett.

'Good point Scarlett. Just to give you the heads up on this – no pun intended – a week ago, Tarn told Scarlett he suspected Trish was having an affair with the head at the school where she works as a teacher. He has no idea how long it's been going on, but he has suspected for a number of weeks and questioned her about it on a number of occasions. It is what has caused them to split up. Following his arrest, he told the interview team that during their row last night she confessed she had been seeing him, and it was at this stage he says he punched the wall and left. As I say we have the physical evidence to back this story up. He has also told the detectives a friend of his saw the pair of then together in a pub.' Pausing she said, 'To answer your question Scarlett, there will be actions to speak with Tarn's friend, regarding the sighting of Trish and the head together and there will be enquiries actioned to visit Trish's school. Questioning the head will be one of those actions.'

Scarlett acknowledged with a nod.

'Finally, I have managed to persuade the command team to leave me in charge of this investigation, even though Tarn is a member of my squad. The approach I will taking will be the same as for any other investigation and that's what I expect you all to do too. The fact that one of our own is a suspect does not alter anything we do. We look for evidence. We prove it's him, we prove it's not him, simple as. We work relentlessly on this because that's what we are trained to do. The other thing I need to point out is that this investigation stays in this room. Speaking to Tarn is strictly off limits. Not because I don't want anybody to talk with him, but because we have to. He will understand. If he were in your shoes he would do the same. I know this is uncomfortable for everyone, but we must act professionally and be beyond reproach.' She scanned the room, 'Yes?'

She received a few nods. 'If anyone is unhappy with that or feels they can't work on this I fully understand and will give you other duties until it is finished. Is everyone okay with that?' She scanned the team. Many of the faces were set tight but the look they returned told her they were on board. Clapping her hands, she said, 'Right, everyone to business then. DI Taylor-Butler will allocate you your tasks.'

There was a scraping back of chairs as people started to rise, ready to start the day.

Thirty-eight

Scarlett had just booted up her computer when a hand on her shoulder made her look up. Diane Harris was standing over her.

She said, 'Are you busy Scarlett?'

'Just making sure I've no urgent e-mails and then I'm making a start, boss.'

'Can I have a word?'

Scarlett pulled away from her keyboard.

'In private please,' Diane added, turning to the door.

Scarlett scooted back her chair, searched for shoes beneath her desk, slipped them on and followed the DCI to her room. By the time she'd caught up, Diane Harris was making herself comfortable behind her desk. She indicated to Scarlett to pull up a chair. The DCI steepled her fingers, a sign Scarlett recognised only too well – this was going to be a talking to.

'The DI tells me you and he have had a few issues while I've been away.'

'Issues?'

'James Green?'

Scarlett huffed. 'I wouldn't say there were issues, boss. You could say we've had a difference of opinion over what Green's been up to, and what he's done since he was released, and I expressed my thoughts on how I felt we should be dealing with him.'

'Nevertheless, he's felt it necessary to bring it to my attention.'

He would do, the arsehole.

'He tells me Green's initiated a formal complaint against you.'

Scarlett nodded, 'Has he told you the circumstances?' She outlined the sighting at the Winstanley Estate, him waving to her at the supermarket, and finally the confrontation she'd had with him at Ella's engagement do at the So Bar, which led to his complaint. 'He set me up boss. I'm convinced Green has been stalking me since his release and I wanted him warning for harassment. That is where DI Taylor-Butler and I have a difference of opinion.' She studied Diane's face a moment before adding, 'I'll be perfectly honest with you, boss, I don't scare easily, you know that, but that night at the So Bar – the look he gave me – that really scared me. I think he's a very dangerous guy.'

The DCI lowered her hands. 'That may be the case Scarlett, and it's something I'm duly noting, but the DI is right in what he says. You can't prove it was him at the Winstanley Estate, and the fact that he waved to you at the supermarket, and you can't disprove what he said about his reason for being at the So Bar – it is a plausible response – does not amount to harassment. And given that he's made a formal complaint against you, which is currently being investigated, I have to tell you to to back off him, unless he does something else that gives us course to pursue.' She met Scarlett's gaze. 'Do I make myself clear?'

Scarlett nodded.

'I'm not taking anyone's side Scarlett, I'm seeing it as it is. The evidence for harassment is not there and you know that, so for now I'm reinforcing what Hayden has already said to you about backing off.' She pushed herself upright in her chair. 'Also, you've got enough on with this investigation.' She held Scarlett's gaze. 'I know how close you and Tarn are, and I just want to reinforce what I said back there at briefing – I don't want you to make contact with him, under any circumstances. If he needs to be seen over anything it will be done by me, do I have your promise on that?'

Scarlett answered with a nod.

'Good. You're a good DS, Scarlett, don't spoil things.'

Scarlett pushed herself up from her seat.

'Oh and one final thing, I've assigned you another partner for now. A DC from Fulham is joining us.' The DCI glanced down at a piece of paper on her desk before smiling. 'Lucy Summers. I've heard good things about her. She's been acting DS for the past six months – she's got a bright future I'm told. Just like you.

I'm sure you'll get on great.' After a pause she said, 'I want you to go back to Tarn's house today and oversee the searches and coordinate the house-to-house. I'll arrange for the new DC to meet you there.'

Scarlett almost let out a frustrated heavy sigh, but caught herself in time, forcing a half-hearted smile before she left.

Thirty-nine

Scarlett was glad to be out of the office. For the past hour, she'd had to suffer DI Taylor-Butler flitting around her, wearing a self-satisfied grin, and it had really pissed her off. And even though she was heading over to the place where a friend of hers had been murdered, it felt like a relief.

The only space she could find to park was a good fifty yards from the outer cordon. The police car that had been blocking the road last night was gone and an officer in high-vis now took its place. She climbed out of the car, pulling on her quilted jacket – the sun was out but there was a sharp chill – and looked up and down the street. There were a few people out but not as many as she anticipated. She'd expected to see some reporters around but there didn't appear to be any, unless they were in nearby houses, door-stepping residents for the juicy angle: After all it was everything you would want in a murder story – the victim covered in blood, their throat cut, and a storyline wrapped in sexual intrigue with a cop as the main suspect. For a moment she stared at the scene, absorbed in silence. It just didn't make sense. She knew Tarn. This was way too brutal. In that instant, her heart fluttered and her stomach turned. She'd had a hollow feeling all the way here thinking about her partner and what had happened to Trish; she knew what it looked like but she refused to believe that Tarn would harm Trish. Any mention of his wife and kids had always been made with the fondest of words. Taking a deep breath, she gathered her thoughts and re-focused. There was lots of activity around the front of Tarn's home; forensic officers had turned their attention to the garden and Task Force officers had started work on the drains, searching for the murder weapon. George and Ella were just going into a house; she knew that they had been assigned door-to-door enquiries.

'DS Macey?'

She spun around. Approaching was a smartly dressed black woman in her mid-twenties in a knee length tan overcoat and patent leather boots. As she neared she flashed a wide grin.

Holding out a hand in greeting she announced, 'DC Summers,' and added, 'Lucy.'

Scarlett took her hand, 'Good to meet you Lucy.' She looked her over. Her immediate thoughts were how pretty she was, admiring her jet black hair set in tight braids and her flawless complexion. 'DCI Harris said you'd be meeting me here.'

Taking away her hand Lucy said, 'Yes I'm so excited. This is my first time on a Homicide Squad, I hardly slept last night.' Then, her face set straight, 'Sorry I didn't mean it to come out like that. To be honest I'm a little bit nervous. This is a big step up for me and I apologise if my enthusiasm has come out wrong. I know you know the victim and the suspect is your partner. I didn't mean to be insensitive.'

Scarlett studied the dark brown eyes. There was a freshness about Lucy that she was already warming to. Inwardly she laughed – a couple of years ago it would have been the type of thing she would have blustered out. She smiled, 'Don't worry, I understand. I've been in a similar situation myself. It's good to have you on board Lucy. Now, I'm told you been acting DS the last six months?'

Lucy nodded, 'Yes, Fulham CID.'

'And you're up to speed with this investigation.'

'DCI Harris filled me in yesterday.'

'Good. Well I want you to coordinate the house-to-house while I liaise with Task Force, who're searching for the knife that killed her.' Turning to the scene she continued, 'There are six of the team doing the house-to-house. I've just seen a couple of my syndicate go into a house three doors down from the victim's home. Make yourself known to them and keep me up to date if anything of interest comes up. Can you do that?'

'Yes, sure thing.'

Scarlett checked her watch, 'We'll come back together here in two hours?'

Lucy took out her mobile to check the time and nodded, 'Two hours, got that.' With a wide grin, she pocketed her phone and marched off toward the uniformed officer protecting the cordon.

Scarlett began to gather her things out of the car before she went to speak to the Task Force Sergeant. Picking her folder off the front seat, she was about to close the car door when movement at the corner of her eye diverted her attention. Thirty yards away, at the road junction and close to a garden hedge, someone dressed in a grey hoodie and jeans was looking her way. Her initial thought was that it was a slim built man, but because the hood was pulled well over their head and a mobile phone held in front of their face, she wasn't sure. What she was certain of was that the person was either photographing or videoing her. James Green jumped into her thoughts and a mix of nervousness coupled with anger overcame her. She looked around for Lucy for support but saw that she was already close to Tarn's house, with her back to her, and the uniform officer guarding the cordon was facing the other way as well. Scarlett decided she had no other choice but to challenge this stranger and took a couple of steps towards them. The person instantly reacted. Scarlett increased her pace and so did they. Then, eyes firmly set on her target, she exploded into a sprint, putting in a burst across the road. The person turned and did the same, making a dash for it and disappearing from view. In the three seconds it took her to make the corner, the stranger had vanished. She stood, trying to catch any sound that might lead her to where the person had scarpered. They had to be in one of the nearby gardens but all she could hear was her own heaving chest. As she cussed, her mobile started ringing.

Forty

'We've found a knife!' It was the Task Force Sergeant.

Catching her breath, but still watching the street to see if the stranger emerged, Scarlett answered 'Give me a minute and I'll be with you.' After ending the call and taking a final look around, she hurried to where task force officers had been lifting drain grates. They were half a dozen houses down from Tarn's, next to an alleyway that looked like a short cut to the next street. Lucy Summers had joined them.

A stocky officer with a blonde crew cut was holding a kitchen knife between the finger and thumb of his gloved hand.

Scarlett eyed it. The knife was the right size and type, but whether it was the murder weapon was difficult to tell because it was covered in silt. Jubilation replaced the frustration she'd felt minutes ago. She acknowledged the find with a nod and the officer dropped it into a clear plastic evidence tube and sealed the top.

Scarlett said, 'Well done, that certainly looks like what we're looking for. Great find. Give it to one of the forensic team, will you, but do further checks in the other drains just to make sure there are no others.' Turning to Lucy she said 'If that is the murder weapon, this alleyway could be where our perp ran. Let's check out where it leads and see what we find. We just might get lucky.'

They had just reached the hedge-lined alley when Scarlett's phone rang again. She fished it of her pocket and viewed the caller ID. It wasn't a number she recognised but she answered anyway. Before she had time to speak, Tarn's voice said her name. She nervously eyed Lucy who was looking at her questioningly, and said, 'Got to take this call,' before moving back into the street and out of earshot. Keeping Lucy in her line of sight she said into her phone, 'You shouldn't be calling me.' She avoided saying her partner's name and though her voice was firm it was also enough for Lucy not to hear. 'What number is this?'

'It's my dad's,' Tarn answered. 'They seized mine last night.'

'We shouldn't be having this conversation.'

'I know and I'm sorry, but I can't just do nothing. They think I killed Trish and I didn't. I need to talk with someone and you're the only person I can trust.'

'I could get in a whole heap of shit for just taking this call.'

'I know and I'm sorry, but you're the only person I can talk to.'

'You're off limits, you know that.'

'Just ten minutes please.'

Scarlett still had her eye on Lucy, who was watching her. She was doing her best to hide the concern she was feeling by smiling every few seconds. For a few seconds, silence reigned as Scarlett's mind went into overdrive. This was her friend and colleague but he was also a suspect in his wife's murder.

'Please Scarlett, ten minutes is all I ask.'

Tarn's insistence dragged back her thoughts. 'Jesus, Tarn you could get me the sack.' Scarlett thought quickly, 'Look, give me half an hour. I'll make some excuse and see you at the coffee bar where we were the other day. But not outside! I can't risk being seen with you. Go upstairs, I'll see you there. And make sure you're not followed.'

Forty-one

Telling Lucy that something important had cropped up, but not elaborating further, she left her to check out the alleyway, and to keep in touch with the search team and house-to-house detectives until she got back. Then, driving as fast as the traffic would allow, she headed to the coffee house. Tarn was waiting in the upstairs seating area, hunched forward on one of the leather sofas, cradling a mug of milky coffee. He looked up and smiled weakly as she approached.

Scarlett couldn't miss the dramatic change to his appearance: he looked like a down-and-out; his complexion was sallow, hair unkempt and he was sporting several day's growth. The T-shirt he wore was creased. As she plonked herself down on the sofa opposite she couldn't help but think that he looked a total wreck.

He dipped his chin to another mug of coffee on the low table that separated them. 'I got you a cappuccino,' he said.

She set down her bag and reached for her drink. 'Thank you.' She studied his face as she took a sip, wondering if this was a bad move. She hoped to God the boss wasn't going to find out.

'Thank you for agreeing to see me Scarlett. I know this could get you into serious trouble.'

It was like he'd read her mind. She put down her coffee. It was lukewarm and she didn't really feel like drinking it. 'Look Tarn, I'll be completely honest, I'm not comfortable with this. Diane Harris has warned us to steer clear of you and I've left the scene to come here.' She decided not to tell him that she'd left her new partner in charge. That would be really rubbing salt into his wounds. 'If I'm found out I'll be off the enquiry.'

'I know, and I'm really grateful to you.' He set down his mug. 'Look I know you need to get back so I'll get straight to the point. I got a phone call this morning from someone who works with Trish at the school who'd heard what had happened.'

Scarlett's eyes widened, 'Oh yes. And?'

'I made some enquiries.'

Screwing up her face she replied, 'You're out of order Tarn. You know that at this stage you're a suspect. This could jeopardise the investigation.'

'Please, just hear me out.' Conscious of his raised voice, he looked around quickly. There were four women at the other end of the room but they didn't glance his way. He continued in a lower tone, 'It's not how it sounds. The person who rang me is the one who tipped me off about Trish in the first place. When I told you about a friend of mine seeing Trish with the head in the pub that time, I wasn't entirely being honest. The person who gave me that info is a teacher at Trish's school. Her name's Sara Bailey.' He stopped for a moment and then continued, 'She rung me at mum and dad's this morning when she couldn't get me on my mobile. Their number is down as an emergency contact. They'd just been told about what happened to Trish. She obviously didn't know what had happened with me.'

'And you chose not to tell her,' Scarlett butted in.

'Look please don't give me the evils Scarlett, I don't need them. What would you have said in the circumstances – oh please don't talk to me I'm on bail because they think I've killed my wife?'

Scarlett took a deep breath, 'You're being facetious Tarn. You know what I mean.'

He sighed, 'Look her phone call took me by surprise. Believe me I didn't ask any questions. She asked me how I was and said they were all really upset. Then she told me Adam hadn't come in this morning and asked if he'd been arrested.'

'Adam?'

'Adam Witton. That's the head's name. The one who's been seeing Trish. Have you arrested him?'

Scarlett shook her head. 'No one's been arrested. We're still processing the scene.' She stopped from telling him at what stage the investigation was at. 'Did she say anything else?'

'No, she just reiterated how sorry everyone was and if I needed anything I could ring her. I told her someone would be coming to the school at some stage and asked her if she was willing to tell you what she'd told me about Trish.'

'And is she?'

He nodded. 'More than willing. She's got no time for Adam at all. She says he's a creep.'

'What does she mean by that?'

'I didn't tell you this before because it wasn't relevant, but now Trish has been killed it is.' He sucked in a deep breath and let it out slowly. 'Adam Witton first tried it on with Sara. It's the reason she rang me about Trish in the first place – she was concerned for her. Sara had been acting as Deputy Head before Adam got the job, and when he was appointed she spent some time with him showing him the procedures and introducing him to staff etcetera. Apparently within weeks he confided in Sara that he hadn't got a good marriage and his wife was mentally ill. Sara said she spent quite a bit of time chatting with him after school because she felt sorry for him, and one evening he asked if she fancied a drink. They went to the pub, and he gave her this sob story about him having no home life – his career was his life – but it got a bit too much for her so suggested they call it a night. He said he'd walk her so far home and then get a taxi, but while they were walking back to her place he tried to kiss her and she had to push him away. She tried to play it down after, at school, but things weren't the same after that – he gave her the cold shoulder, sidelining her from the Ofsted visit, and that's when she noticed he was spending a lot of time with Trish.' Tarn frowned, 'Sara tried to warn Trish about him, and Trish denied anything was going on, but when she saw them together in the pub she rang me to warn me about him.' He broke off again. 'It looks as though Trish fell for his spiel and this how their relationship developed. You know the rest from our conversations.'

His eyes started to water. 'Gosh what a mess. I'm sorry for you Tarn.'

Tight-lipped he said, 'A big fucking mess Scarlett, but I didn't kill her. I swear. I went round last night to try and sort it out. I got angry with her and she told me I didn't make her happy any more and Adam was more a man than me. Sure I fucking lost it when she said that, but I didn't touch her. Fuck me, I wanted to, but I punched the wall instead and left.' He shook his head, 'I'm telling you as a friend Scarlett, Trish was alive when I left. I didn't kill her.'

'So what are you thinking? Adam Witton?'

'I can only think of him. Especially with Sara telling me he's not turned up at school this morning. It certainly looks suspicious, don't you think? It's something you can follow up. Have you got anything from the neighbours? Surely they saw someone other than me. That street is not exactly busy – it's not a short cut or anything.'

Scarlett took a deep breath, 'You know I can't tell you what evidence we've got Tarn. That's unfair.'

Tarn nodded, 'Yes I know. I didn't mean it like that. It was a comment, not a question. At least I've given you another starting point.'

'When I get back to the nick I'll ring the school and make arrangements to see this Sara Bailey. In the meantime, you avoid talking to her any more. I'll make it look to the gaffer as though I've come by this information from my enquiries.'

Tarn reached across and touched the back of Scarlett's hand, 'This is fucking crucifying me Scarlett. My wife's been murdered and I can't even see my kids because I'm being treated as a suspect. Do you know what that's like? Even my fucking mum and dad are looking at me suspiciously.' Suppressing a sob, he wiped a tear from his eye. 'Please get them Scarlett. Get whoever killed Trish, won't you? For me.'

Forty-two

Scarlett decided Tarn's information was far too important to leave for that evening's briefing and so she rang the incident room, concocting a story that the deputy head at Trish's school had rang her direct, asked to see her urgently and she was on her way over there now. Then she turned off her phone and drove back to Brentford, to the school where Trish worked.

At reception, Scarlett learned Sara Bailey was filling in again as Deputy Head, and within minutes she saw the teacher coming along the corridor. A little on the plump side, Sara was a pretty woman with long dark hair, in her late thirties, who looked anxious.

'This is really shocking news. Everyone is devastated about Trish. She was a lovely person,' she said. Pointing down the corridor, she added, 'We can talk in the staff room.'

Neither woman spoke as they made their way to the staff room. The only sounds were muted voices of children coming from nearby classrooms.

The staff room was empty. Closing the door behind them, Sara asked, 'Can I get you a drink?'

Scarlett shook her head. 'To be honest I should be back at the scene. I'm here because Tarn has told me you rang him this morning...'

'Yes, to offer him our condolences...' Interrupted Sara, offering a seat to Scarlett, 'And just to let him know we're here for him, if he needs anything. But I guess he's got all the support he needs from his family and work.'

Scarlett felt a knot in her stomach. She wasn't about to tell Sara he was currently their only suspect and suspended from work. She said, 'He's taking a few days out at the moment, so he can sort things.'

'Yes, I guess he needs to. I can't imagine what he's going through. I know they have two young children. This really is so shocking.'

There was a couple of seconds silence, almost as if they were honouring the memory of Trish. She broke the quiet by saying, 'Tarn told me you rang him to tell him about Trish and the head…'

'Adam Witton. Yes,' she broke into Scarlett's sentence again. Her mouth tightened momentarily, 'It was a real dilemma for me. Has Tarn told you about the time Adam tried it on with me not long after he was appointed?'

Scarlett nodded.

'We spent quite a bit of time together when he first started six months ago, you know, showing him how the school functioned, introducing him to staff, blah-de-blah. Then one evening he started telling me about his personal life – that his wife had a few mental health issues. I thought he just wanted to get things off his chest and needed someone to talk through his problems, so when he asked me if I'd go to the pub with him for a drink I didn't see anything wrong in it. Even when he offered to walk me part of the way home, we were chatting so I didn't think anything of it. So when he tried to kiss me it took me completely by surprise. He tried to make light of it when I asked him what he was doing. And he apologised and said he'd read my signals all wrong. Afterwards I did get to thinking about it, and I came to the conclusion that he had been spinning me a yarn, to make me feel sorry for him, hoping I'd fall for it. After that I was guarded and professional around him, and it was a couple of weeks later when I spotted he was spending quite a bit of time with Trish and noticed there seemed to be a little closeness between them. I've known Trish a long time – we're good friends as well as colleagues – and so one evening after school, when there was only me and her, I told her that I noticed her and Adam were spending a lot of time together. She laughed it off by saying there wasn't anything going on between them, if that was what I was thinking – she was just helping him with the Ofsted visit. Then I saw them together in the pub having a drink.

You could see by their body language it was more than a drink together.' Pausing a moment and locking eyes with Scarlett she added, 'It wasn't by accident I caught them. Because of what had happened to me with Adam I kept a close watch on the pair, and I noticed that on a couple of occasions they were making an excuse to hang back after everyone had gone home, and so one evening I parked up on the street outside and waited for them to come out, and that's when I saw Adam and Trish get into his car and I followed them to the pub.' She took in a deep breath. 'I spent a good few days mulling things over what I'd seen before I finally decided to ring Tarn. And I didn't ring him to stir things up between them, or cause damage to their marriage, but because of what I'd found out had gone on at his other school. I was concerned for Trish.'

Alerted by her last sentence Scarlett sprang up from her slouch, 'What had gone on at his other school?'

Sara took in another deep breath, held it for a couple of seconds and then released it heavily. 'I didn't tell Tarn this, but an old friend of mine was a teacher at his last school – he was the head of a primary at Wembley – and she told me that when he left, it was under a cloud. I made the call because I was suspicious about him – you know the story he'd given me and what was happening with Trish – I wanted to know if he'd done anything similar at his last school…'

'And had he?' It was Scarlett's turn to cut into their conversation.

Trish nodded. 'My friend told me he'd had an affair with a teacher at her school and that the teacher concerned had to leave. She was married. The affair came out because a load of damage had been done to her car. She'd had her tyres slashed and paint stripper thrown over it. And a brick was thrown through her window at home one night. It all happened after she'd ended it between them. The husband called the police and Adam was interviewed about it all. He'd denied it and the police were unable to prove anything. The teacher concerned handed in her notice, and he'd applied for the Head vacancy at our school and got it.'

'Weren't the Governors aware when they appointed him?'

Sara shrugged her shoulders. 'No, we weren't. I was on the panel that interviewed him. He was easily the best candidate and came with a good reference. When I spoke to my friend, the deputy at his last school, she told me they had taken advice, after he'd told them he'd got the job here, but they couldn't put anything in about it because he'd not been charged. We never thought to ring the school before we appointed him. It was only after he'd tried it on with me, and what I believed was happening with Trish, that I made the call.'

'Wow, that's thrown a spanner in the works.'

'I just thought because of what happened to that other teacher and this with Trish – not for one minute am I wanting to suggest Adam killed her, but you know, especially with him not turning into school this morning, I thought it was important you should know.'

Scarlett leaned forward, 'You've done the right thing Sara. Adam not being here might be completely innocent. He might be ill or something. But I need to chase it up all the same.' She stood up.

Sara started to rise, 'He's not at home. Or at least he wasn't when I rang just after nine this morning and spoke to his wife. She said he hadn't come home last night and she didn't know where he was. I tried his mobile and it went through to voicemail. I've left him a message to contact me.'

Scarlett took out her notebook and pen, scribbled down Sara's full details, Adam Witton's address and the name of the teacher Adam had the affair with at his previous school, and then snatching up her bag, sought out her BlackBerry and switched it back on. She shook hands with Sara and thanked her, told her she would be back to take a statement and left the staff room. With a spring in her step she strode across the playground, putting in a call to Diane Harris.

The DCI answered on the third ring. Before she had time to say anything Scarlett said excitedly, 'Boss, can you meet me at Tarn's? I think I've got a strong lead.'

Forty-three

Scarlett met DCI Diane Harris outside Tarn's house. Lucy Summers joined them. Scarlett stuck to the same story she'd told the incident room earlier, avoiding steady eye contact with either of them, hoping it wasn't going to backfire on her. She related Sara Bailey's tale with the same detail as she'd been given.

When she finished, Diane Harris said, 'You were right, this couldn't wait for evening briefing Scarlett. We need to act on this straight away.'

Scarlett breathed a sigh of relief. The response was music to her ears. 'We need to go to Adam Witton's home and see if he's there. If it's as his wife told Sara – that she hasn't seen him since last night – we need to find out if she knows where he is and we could also do with searching the place.'

'Totally agree Scarlett. I want you and Lucy to get over there and take George and Ella as back up. If Adam Witton's at home, bring him in, and if you find anything suspicious at his house, secure the place and call out forensics.'

***

Witton's home was in Northolt. The two-bedroom semi-detached house, built shortly after the war, had a red-brick ground floor and cream coloured stucco to the upper storey. It lay at the head of a cul-de-sac, and had a low front wall and freshly mown small lawn. To the right was a driveway which led to a side door and a concrete garage with double wooden doors that looked to be 1940s original.

Scarlett and Lucy walked up the concrete drive. George Martin and Ella Bloom had stayed in the back of the car, in view, at the bottom of the drive, waiting while Scarlett made the introductions and broke the ice.

She pressed the side doorbell and waited. It didn't take Mrs Witton long to answer. She was a thin, wiry woman, with long brown hair and dark brown eyes. She wore a floral top and jeans. Scarlett took in her well made-up face and rich red painted fingernails – she didn't look like a woman with mental health issues. Scarlett held up her identification and introduced herself and Lucy and asked if her husband was at home.

She eyed them suspiciously. 'I'm afraid he isn't.'

Scarlett thought she sounded nervous. 'Do you know where he is, Mrs Witton?'

'No, I don't…' she broke off, studied the pair for a moment and then said, 'Do you mind if I ask what this is about?'

'We want to speak with him as a matter of importance.'

'Well I'm afraid, as I said, he isn't here.'

'Do you know where he is?'

'No, I don't. I thought he was at school. He's the head of a primary school in Brentford, but I know he isn't there. The school contacted me this morning to tell me he hadn't arrived.'

'When did you last see your husband?'

'Why are you asking all these questions? I've told you I don't know where he is.'

Mrs Witton was starting to get anxious. Scarlett softened the formality of her tone with her reply. 'It is important we speak with him. Have you any idea at all where he might be?'

'None. And in response to your last question I haven't seen him since last evening. After his meal, he said that he had to go out – that he had some school business to attend to – and he left in his car. I haven't seen him since. Look, do you mind if I ask what this is about. Is he in trouble or something?'

'May we come in for a moment?' Without waiting for a response Scarlett put a foot on the threshold and stepped up into the doorway, forcing Mrs Witton to take a stride back. For a moment it looked as if the woman was going to challenge her, but then she lowered her gaze, and with a sigh of resignation turned aside and let them in.

The kitchen Scarlett and Lucy walked into looked in need of a makeover. The wooden cupboards and tiles above the work surfaces were years out of date, though the place was tidy. Scarlett looked around the room, stopping her gaze by the integrated cooker and hob. A wooden knife block stood next to it. The black handles of the knives were the only thing visible and they looked to be of the same style as the one found that morning. One of the slots was empty – her heart started beating fast and she felt a rush of adrenalin. 'Mrs Witton, can we go through to the lounge?'

Forty-four

'Adam Witton's done a runner.' Scarlett was at the bottom of the Wittons' driveway speaking on her BlackBerry to Diane Harper. She'd already told her DCI about the missing knife from the wooden block in the kitchen. 'We've seized and bagged the knife block, and I've got George and Ella going through the house now for details of Adam's car. As soon as we get his registration I'll text it to the incident room. And Lucy is talking to Alice Witton. It looks like she and Adam have had a fight or he's attacked her before he left. She's got marks to her neck and arms. She's not saying too much at the moment but she's admitted they had a row yesterday evening and he stormed out. She says she's no idea where he is. We've got his mobile number, and we're going through with her the list of friends and family, or places he's likely to go, to see if we can narrow down where he is. Once that's compiled I'll ring everything in.'

'Splendid job Scarlett,' the DCI replied, 'I'll get a forensic team over to you as soon as possible. What about Alice Witton? What are you doing about her?'

'Understandably she's a bit shell-shocked by it all. She's asked us why we're searching her place and so we've told her we want to speak to him about Trish's murder. She went a bit hysterical at first but she's calmed down a bit now. I'm going to give it another half an hour and then get her across to a victim suite with Lucy and interview her. I'll get an FME out to examine her injuries, and get a CSI officer to photograph and swab them. I'm leaving George and Ella at the house to liaise with forensics.'

'Well it looks as though you've got things pretty much sewn up. The minute you get hold of Adam's car's details let us know and we can get the ball rolling to try and locate it.'

'Will do boss.' Scarlett ended the call and returned to the house.

***

Diane Harris took the evening briefing. The murder board behind her was now three-quarters full of images, intelligence and timeline information. A photograph of the knife recovered that morning was up there too, together with a recent photo of Adam Witton – supplied by his wife Lucy – and an image of a red 3 series BMW with the registration number of Adam's car. She tapped Adam's photo, 'We've carried out a number of checks this afternoon at addresses of close family members and friends of Adam Witton without success, and we've now circulated his photograph, together with details of his car. If he passes any of the road network cameras we'll get an instant hit. We've also locked onto his phone. It's deactivated at the moment so we can't get a location, but the minute he uses it we'll get him.' She looked across to Scarlett. 'Tell the team what you and Lucy got from his wife this afternoon.'

Scarlett straightened in her seat. 'Lucy and I interviewed Alice Witton this afternoon. It took us quite a bit of time to get her to open up. I don't think it was because she was protecting him or anything, but she was overwhelmed by it all and embarrassed. She said she'd known Adam had been having affairs with several women for the best part of eighteen months because she'd found some dating sites in the history on his laptop. She challenged him about them, and they'd had several rows. Six months ago, after another heated argument in which she'd threatened divorce, he'd confessed he'd met a couple of women from the dating site but nothing had happened.' She caught the wry smiles on the faces of many syndicate members. Suppressing a grin she continued, 'Although Adam has a well-paid job, Lucy and I discovered the home and most of the money in the bank account belongs to Mrs Witton, inherited following her grandparent's death. He'd promised after their last argument, six months ago, that there would be no more seeing other women. She thought getting this head's job had stopped it all but then she found some texts on his phone two days ago from Trish Scarr, which made her suspect he was having another affair, and last night they'd rowed about it and he told her he was leaving. He left the house shortly after six p.m.' She looked around the table. The squad had latched on to the significance of this time-frame: it easily gave Adam Witton the time to drive across to the Scarr household, murder Trish and leave before the neighbour found her body. He could well have got there, seen Tarn leaving the house and then gone in. Why he'd killed her was another question, and one they would only have answered once they had him in custody. She continued, 'We didn't mention the affair with the teacher at his last school because we didn't want to compound her torment and anyway we've only got what Sara Bailey has told us at the moment. We now know the teacher he was involved with is called Helen Davis. The mobile number Sara gave us for Helen is no longer in use so I contacted the school where she and Adam last worked. I spoke with the new head there, a Mrs McDonald, and she told me Helen had already left prior to her being appointed and she believes she is now working at a school in Golders Green. She also said Helen had moved house. She's going to make some phone calls on our behalf and get back to me tomorrow. Once we track Helen Davis down we'll go and talk to her about what happened between her and Adam and the damage to her car and house.'

'And the injuries to Alice Witton?' asked the Diane Harris.

'Yes, to her neck and arms. The Force Medical Officer who examined her describes them as scratch and grab marks. She's also had some of her hair pulled out. We asked her about how she'd come by them and she said when Adam had told her he was leaving she'd grabbed his car keys to try and stop him and he'd attacked her to get them back.' Pausing again, she added, 'It certainly gives us an insight into his frame of mind when he left his house.'

Diane Harris nodded. 'It certainly does.' She switched her gaze between Scarlett and Lucy Summer. 'Thank you for that. Good work you two today.' Then taking back briefing she continued, 'There's nothing much else we can do for now. Alice Witton wanted to go back home, so I've put a uniform officer with her tonight in case Adam shows his face, though I don't think he will. It's been plastered all over the news today, and he's not daft – my guess is he's lying low until he can sort things out – maybe ditch any incriminating evidence. He'd have been covered in blood, so he needs to get rid of his clothing for one.' She clapped her hands, 'Good work everybody. Now I see a lot of tired faces, so time for home guys and we'll start afresh tomorrow.'

Forty-five

Scarlett dumped the empty coffee cartons from her desk into the bin and had just started to tidy away her paperwork when her mobile rang. It was Alex. She recalled their last time together and a warm feeling engulfed her. She snatched it up and answered.

'What're you doing?' Alex asked.

'Just finishing work.'

'Still on your partner's wife's case?'

'Still. But we've had a breakthrough today. We've got a new suspect.'

'Don't tell me, the butler did it.'

She burst out laughing.

'Fancy going for a drink?'

Her stomach fluttered and her heart did a double beat. The sensation reminded her of when they had first started seeing one another. 'I'd love to say yes, but I'm all sweaty, and in my work clothes and I've come to work on the bike. I'll have to go home first – it's going to be a good hour at least before I'm presentable.'

'I like sweaty. Sweaty on you is good from my recollections.'

She caught the suggestive note in his voice. 'Alex King, that is sexism in the workplace, that is.'

'I'm not in your workplace.' After a couple of seconds, he said, 'Look, forget the going out. Why don't you come straight over to my place and get cleaned up here? I'll rustle us up some supper – what do you say?'

'That's sounds like an offer I can't refuse.'

'Good, see you in about half an hour – yes?'

'Definitely, yes.'

***

Alex's apartment was on the third floor of a refurbished 1930s block in Twickenham. He had his own parking space, which was an end slot, so there was enough room for Scarlett to park her bike beside his Range Rover Sport without encroaching on someone else's space. Taking off her helmet she shook out her red hair, ruffled her fingers through it to tease out the knots and then strode across to the entrance where she pressed Alex's intercom. He buzzed her in and she rode the lift, partly unzipping the top half of her biking leathers, suddenly overcome by the warmth of the building. His door was already open and he was standing in the entrance as she exited the lift. He was dressed in a tight-fitting T-shirt and jeans and again she felt her heart speed up a notch as she approached him.

'It's a long time since I've had a sexy girl come to my apartment dressed in leather.'

Scarlett giggled, pushing her helmet into his arms. 'And that's as close as you're getting Alex King. All I want is a glass of wine.'

'Don't I even get a little kiss?'

She shook her head disapprovingly, then leant in and kissed his lips. She felt his mouth open slightly, hinting at a longer kiss but she pulled back and smiled, pushing past him. 'That's it lover boy. Now where's my drink?'

Alex let out a laugh as he closed the door, then headed across the lounge to the kitchen.

The room was open plan, the décor in keeping with the 30s building – furnishings of dark leather, chrome and Perspex were art deco style, and on the walls were prints of 1930s movie posters together with memorabilia and photos from Alex's army days. Scarlett was always in awe when she visited his place because the furnishings in her home had belonged to her Aunt Hanna and were showing signs of wear. Even the décor, magnolia walls and white doors, was her aunt's taste. Except for a three-seater sofa, a double bed and a smart TV, she hadn't replaced anything. Taking in the surroundings while pulling off her boots, she decided she needed to make some changes this year. Placing her boots against the skirting she shrugged off her biking suit and dropped it beside them.

Alex had taken a bottle of white wine from the fridge. At the kitchen island he uncorked it, poured two glasses and then passed her a glass, chinking it and saying, 'cheers.'

Scarlett took a generous swallow. The chill instantly refreshed her mouth and the after-notes of pear and lemon were a delight to her taste buds. This was a good wine. 'That really has hit the spot,' she said. 'You know how to treat a girl.'

'Only the best for the best.'

She felt herself blush, which surprised her, and Alex gave a wicked smile.

'It's a long time since I've made anyone blush. I must be getting smoother in my old age.'

Scarlett blushed even deeper and punched his arm. 'Stop it now Alex.'

He laughed and moved back into the kitchen space. 'I've put some chicken, with goat's cheese, wrapped in parma ham in the oven, and I'm just about to boil some new potatoes and put some veg on. Do you want to grab a shower and then we'll eat?'

'I'd love to take a shower, if you don't mind, but you'll have to put up with me back in my work clothes.'

'Why don't you borrow a pair of my joggers and a T shirt?'

She looked at him.

'Straight up. You'll be far more comfortable and it's not as though you haven't done it before. You know where everything is.'

'Are you sure?'

'Absolutely. Make yourself at home.'

Scarlett used the shower in Alex's en-suite and picked out a white T-shirt and a pair of grey jogging bottoms from his wardrobe. She had to tie the waistband as tight as she could, letting them rest on her hips, to stop them falling down. Then, scrunching her hair in a towel she stepped back into the lounge.

Alex was at the island dishing up their meal. The wine glasses had been replenished and he'd put on some music. She recognised *Hello*, the opening track from Adele's *25* album. Scarlett finished off mopping most of the wet from her hair and set the towel down on the worktop. She picked up one of the glasses. 'This is really good of you Alex,' she said and took a drink.

'Like I said earlier, never say I don't know how to treat a girl.' Picking up the steaming plates and nodding towards his laid-out table he added, 'Come on let's not let this go cold. The remainder of the bottle is in the fridge if you want to get it.'

Forty-six

Scarlett loaded Alex's dishwasher with the empty plates while he opened another bottle of wine. They had spent their meal talking about Trish's murder. She'd mentioned her clandestine meeting with Tarn and he'd offered her words of support, 'I think I'd have done the same if it was my partner.' It made her feel better. And she'd told him about Adam Witton, knowing he would keep what she'd disclosed to himself. As always she'd asked him what he'd been up to, and as usual he hadn't given anything away, merely told he'd been doing this and that – nothing of interest. The look he'd given her told Scarlett he was toying with her again, and she'd threatened that one day she was going to find out what he did for a living – even if she had to torture him. He'd laughed, telling her, he might enjoy it. It had been like old times.

Pushing in the stacked shelves and closing the dishwasher door she turned to see Alex holding out a full glass for her. He was flashing that trademark smile of his and his sparkling blue eyes were locked on. Suddenly, what felt like an electric current, tingled through her – she hadn't felt like this for a long while. She took the glass, but instead of taking a drink, set it down on the island and leaned in for a kiss. Pressing her mouth to his, she gently bit his bottom lip and probed with her tongue. He pulled her to him, sliding his hands beneath the T- shirt she was wearing, running them up her back and along her ribs. She stiffened, her body tingling, and she hungrily kissed him deeper, clawing her fingers through his dark hair. She felt his hardness pushing against her and gasped. Pulling back her head, but still holding him in a clinch, she met his eyes. She didn't say anything, and neither did he, but they didn't need to: They were both burning with desire for one another. Alex grabbed her wrist and pulled her towards the bedroom.

***

In the darkness of Alex's flat, wearing only his T-shirt, Scarlett stood in front of the floor-to-ceiling window and stared down at the street below. It was almost midnight but still a steady flow of traffic trundled along the road. It had rained while they were in bed and car headlights blazed their reflections back off the damp surface, obscuring the edges, giving the illusion that one vehicle melded into the next, forming an endless red and white moving light-stream. Her thoughts drifted back to the last hour. The sex had been great, as if they had never been apart. And it had reminded her of how things had been between them – before she had decided to end it. *Why?*

Padded footfalls behind her grabbed her attention back to the present and she glanced over her shoulder, catching Alex creeping towards her. He wrapped his arms around her waist and pulled her into him, settling his chin into the nape of her neck, then he gently kissed her and she felt herself melt. 'That's nice,' she muttered.

'I wondered where you'd gone.'

'Just chilling. Watching the traffic.'

'Was I that boring?'

She gave him a half-laugh. 'You were good. Amazing.'

'So were you.' He kissed her neck again and gave her a squeeze. 'Do you want to give it another go between us?'

Forty-seven

In his flat James Green sat in semi darkness, his eyes reflecting the light from his laptop screen. He was viewing the video he'd downloaded that morning. He froze the image at the moment where Detective Macey had clocked him, though he could see by the look on her face she hadn't recognised him. Inwardly he smiled, but then panic overcame him. She had almost caught him – if it hadn't been for the nearby houses and gardens! He hadn't realised just how quick she was – he had only seen her jogging before today. He'd have to be more careful in future.

Breathing deeply to steady his racing heart, he clicked on the right mouse button, selected 'print' from the drop-down menu and waited for it to come out of the printer. Picking out the A4 image, he gave it another look, and then stood and went over to the wall to add it to the gallery. Choosing the spot carefully, he taped it up, and took a step back, studying his collection of photographs like an art connoisseur. He had quite a nice portfolio of his targets. Soon, he told himself, it will be your turn. But not just yet!

Forty-eight

Scarlett was awake long before the alarm went off on her phone. For the past ten minutes she had lain there, listening to Alex's steady breathing, a smile on her face that an atom bomb wouldn't remove. When her alarm did go off it made her jump.

Alex stirred.

'It's for me. Work,' she said gently, casting aside her half of the duvet and picking up her mobile, deactivating the trilling sound.

She showered and changed back into the clothes she'd worn the previous day. They were creased, but only slightly, and, thankfully, the smell they carried was nothing more than a hint of her delicate Elie Saab perfume, for which she was grateful. It meant she could go onto work from here without the need for a detour home to change into something fresh. It also meant she had time for coffee and toast.

She made herself a hot drink and a round of toast and devoured both standing in front of the huge windows. Twickenham had woken up – the traffic was already building, heading into the city and it wasn't even 7 a.m. Another half an hour and it would be snarled. That was why she was so glad she had the bike for her commute – in the main it allowed her freer passage through the constant jams. She finished her breakfast, put her mug into Alex's dishwasher, brewed him a coffee and returned to the bedroom. He was awake. She set down the steaming coffee on his bedside table and leaned over to kiss him. He took her by surprise, grabbing hold of her, dragging her down onto the bed, smothering her with an open-mouth kiss. She playfully fought herself free. 'Some of us have to go to work.'

He let out a short laugh. 'See you tonight?' He asked.

'No work today?'

'I've got a meeting at eleven, and lunch with a couple of colleagues and that's my day.'

'All right for some.' She replied, pushing herself up. 'I'll ring you as soon I know what's happening. If we get Adam Witton it could be a long one.'

'Okay no probs.'

Flashing him a wide happy smile, she blew a kiss, said 'Thanks for last night,' and after one last, lingering look she left the bedroom.

***

Scarlett parked Bonnie in the rear yard, ran up the station's back stairs, and headed to the ladies to take off her motorcycle gear and make herself presentable. She was just refreshing her eye make-up when her personal mobile rang. Laying aside her eye liner she took the phone out of her bag and viewed the screen. It was the number Tarn had rung her from yesterday. She sighed and turned her attention to the three toilet cubicles. All of them were open. She answered in a quiet voice, 'You shouldn't be ringing me.'

'I know but I got a call from Sara yesterday. She told me you'd been to see her. Have you got him?'

'Tarn, this is unfair.'

'I promise I won't ring you any more. Just tell me if you've got him?'

'Not yet. Look, all I can tell you is that we have circulated him. We have no idea where he is but we're pulling out all the stops to find him. I'm just going into briefing so I'll get an update. The moment I get anything I can tell you, I promise I'll ring you.'

'Please Scarlett, this is killing me.'

'I promise Tarn, I will.'

She ended the call and stared at her phone. It was hard to imagine what her partner was going through – his wife dead, unable to see his two kids, though until they got Adam Witton, he was still a suspect and she had to be careful what she said. Sometimes this job was so unfair.

Forty-nine

Mug of freshly made coffee in hand, Scarlett studied the incident board. There had been a couple of additions overnight – a short asterisk note to trace Helen Davis – the teacher Adam Witton had an affair with at his last school: this morning, Scarlett was hoping to learn where she lived or worked, so they could pay her a visit. There was also the CSI evidential photograph of Alice Witton, taking during her examination by The Force Medical Examiner, with a list of her injuries penned down the side. Adam's status had gone from 'suspect' to 'wanted.'

The sudden, noisy, opening of the squad room door made her look around. Diane Harris and Hayden Taylor-Butler strode in, heading for the incident board to start briefing. Stepping aside, Scarlett gave them a quick smile and returned to her desk. Around the room, members of the team looked up from what they were doing and fell silent.

The DCI dimmed the lights and activated the large video screen next to the board. An aerial view of a built-up area with a winding river jumped into focus. With a pen beam she threw a red dot on a building close to the edge of the waterway, in the shadow of a bridge carrying a main road. 'This, guys, is The Dissenters' Chapel at Kensal Green All Souls Cemetery, close to the Grand Union Canal. An hour ago Adam Witton's BMW was found abandoned here. The back seats were heavily bloodstained.' The team stirred. 'Adam Witton was not with his vehicle and there's no sign of him. Officers are down there now securing the area and I've got a team of forensics attending as we speak. I'm diverting Task Force to the scene to begin a search of the area.' She nodded to Scarlett, 'I want you to go there straight after briefing and oversee the search of the location and the recovery of Adam's vehicle.'

'Yes boss,' said Scarlett.

'This is what we've been waiting for. I've arranged for footage to be viewed from cameras all along the route, to and from the cemetery. We don't know if he has another vehicle or not – according to his wife he hasn't, so he most probably will have left here on foot. The towpath beside the canal goes all the way through to Paddington, so I'm arranging for checks to be made from everywhere it comes out onto the main road, right to the station, just in case he's boarded a train. I've put an alert on his debit and credit cards and we're monitoring his phone.' The DCI started listing actions pertinent to the discovery and began allocating them to the team. Scarlett's new partner, Lucy Summers, was given the job of baby-sitting Alice Witton, to check if she could give other information as to Adam's possible whereabouts and to report back immediately if he made contact: they were not expecting him to return home anytime soon but he just might make a telephone call. She ended the briefing by stating any DNA results from Trish and Tarn's home were going to be at least another 24 hours; the labs had prioritised them, but they were still in a queue. Then turning off the screen she checked if anyone had any questions, wished everyone good hunting and left with the DI.

Scarlett slurped the remains of her coffee down in a gulp and scribbled down the telephone number of Adam's previous school, so she could speak to the new head, Mrs McDonald, about Helen Davis. She stuffed her notebook into her bag, picked up a set of keys for one of the pool cars and breezed out of the office.

Fifty

Wearing a forensic onesie, Scarlett stayed the sterile side of the blue and white tape, watching three CSI officers going about their work around Adam Witton's red BMW. It lay abandoned thirty yards away down a gentle slope, close to the old Dissenters' Chapel – a Gothic style building, refurbished into a tea room for visitors to the well-known cemetery. It was Scarlett's first visit to the place and the beautiful surroundings captivated her. Entering the magnificent gates to gain access, she was surprised she had never noticed the place before, despite having driven past it many times. The cemetery was closed to visitors today. The entrance had been sealed off and the only people around the place were police officers.

All four doors and the boot to Adam's car were open. One of the CSI team was taking photographs of its interior. Task Force had also arrived and they were currently being briefed on the towpath prior to the start of their search. Scarlett would catch up with the supervisors of both teams as soon as they made themselves available. She took out her BlackBerry and dialled the number for Adam's previous school. In less than a minute she was speaking with Mrs McDonald, who informed her that she had already left her a message on her phone at work. Scarlett thanked her, told her she was out of the office, and wouldn't be back until a lot later in the day and asked if she would mind repeating the message. The head had tracked down Helen Davis to Wessex Gardens Primary School in Golders Green and had already spoken with her, told her what it was about and had to expect a call from Scarlett. Helen was more than happy to discuss Adam Witton. Scarlett thanked Mrs McDonald, took down the number of Wessex Gardens Primary and ended the call. Then, she rang the school. The girl on reception told her Helen was presently teaching her class but she would ask Helen to ring at morning break, in five minutes.

Not long, thought Scarlett, ending the call and she returned her attention to the scene. The three CSI team members were huddled around something a few yards away from Adam's BMW. She couldn't see what it was, but they had set a yellow numbered pyramid marker next to it. Curiosity piqued, she drew up her hood and face-mask, ducked underneath the crime-scene tape and set off down the track to join them.

Halfway down the slope her BlackBerry rang. Stopping, she pulled it out of her pocket and answered.

It was a nervous sounding Helen Davis asking if that was DS Macey? 'I've been told you want to talk to me about Adam Witton?' she said.

Scarlett took a deep breath. This had caught her on the hop. 'Oh hi Helen, yes you're right. Have you been told what it's about?'

'Mrs McDonald rang me this morning, but I've also spoken with Sara Bailey, who I know you've interviewed and she's given me some more details. She said you think he might have killed a teacher at her school?'

For a few seconds Scarlett didn't respond. Choosing her words carefully she answered, 'That might not be the case Helen. We certainly want to talk to Adam in relation to the death of a teacher he worked with and at the moment we're trying to trace him.' After pausing a second, she added, 'You wouldn't happen to know where he is or where he might go by any chance, would you?'

'No idea.'

'Can I ask when you last saw him, or were in contact with him?'

There was a moment's silence before she responded, 'It would be about six months ago now. You're probably aware I went off sick for a while after what happened between Adam and me, and then Adam got the head's job at the school where Sara Bailey works. I haven't seen him since he left.'

'I don't want to embarrass you Helen, but I've been told you and Adam had a bit of a thing going when he was at your school.'

There was a few seconds of nothing again before she answered, 'Yes we had a brief affair. I know Sara's told you.'

'She didn't tell me that to stir things up for you, Helen. She thought it might be relevant to what has happened to her friend and colleague Trish Scarr. You see Trish was also having an affair with Adam at the school where they worked together.'

'Yes, Sara's told me.'

'I want to come and see you about what occurred between you and Adam, and get a statement, if I may, but I'm a bit tied up at the moment so is it all right if I talk over the phone for now?'

'I've only got about ten minutes. Then I'm back in class.'

'That's okay I only want to ask you a couple of questions.' Quickly composing herself Scarlett continued, 'You and Adam – how did it start?'

'I guess it was one of those things that just crept up. Adam was a nice guy. We all knew he had issues with his wife. You know, mental health problems...'

'How did you find out about those issues?' Scarlett interrupted.

'From Adam. It was no secret. It sometimes affected his work. Coping with her used to get him down. He used to sometimes mention it in the staff room when things had gone off between them.'

'You mean when they'd had a row?'

'Sometimes it was more than that. She attacked him.'

'Oh!?'

'Yes, a couple of times he came to work with his face all scratched and he told us she'd gone off on one again."

'What did he say was wrong with his wife?'

'He told us she was bipolar.'

'Did you believe him?'

'Of course. Why? Is that not the case?'

She sounded shocked. 'To be honest I don't know,' said Scarlett. 'Sara Bailey also mentioned something about his wife's mental state, which is something we're following up on.' After letting that sink in, she added, 'So how did you and Adam get together?'

'As I said, it just crept up. We used to chat quite a lot. Then, we'd all go out as a group from school, and then it got to just me and him going out for a drink. My marriage was going through a bad patch at the time and it just happened between us. It wasn't something we planned.'

Not for you it might not have been, thought Scarlett, thinking about Adam trying it on with Sara Bailey and this recent episode with Trish. And then there were the dating sites Adam's wife had told them about. She asked, 'How long were you and he together?'

'It wasn't long. A couple of months. Me and Graham, that's my husband, split up for a short time but we sorted our differences out and I told Adam I wanted to call it a day.'

'And how did Adam react?'

'He was upset initially and he begged me to carry things on between us. He said he would leave his wife, but I didn't really believe him, and things had improved between Graham and I, so I told him no.'

'I've been told your car was damaged. Did that happen after you told Adam it was off between you?'

'Yes, within a matter of days. I left work one evening and all the tyres had been slashed and paint stripper thrown over the bonnet. It cost me a fortune because I wasn't covered for malicious damage.'

'And did you challenge Adam about it?'

'Yes, the moment I found it like that. I went back into the school and asked him if it was him.'

'And what did he say?'

'Just denied it. I told him I was calling the police. He told me not to, that he'd sort it, but I was furious. I called them and also spoke to my union. The union advised me to go off sick and I know the police interviewed him because they came back and told me he'd denied it and he had an alibi. Two nights later the lounge window at our house was smashed. A brick was thrown through it. We called the police again and I told them about Adam. I'd already told Graham about us. They said they'd talk to Adam, but without any witnesses their hands were tied as to what they could do. That's when I decided to go for the job I'm doing now and hand in my notice. I'd had enough of the hassle and I didn't want any more. It was a shame because I loved working at that school. I'd started my career there. Colleagues told me Adam had been spoken to by the Governors and he was applying for another post, but it was too late by then for me. And of course, as you know, he's now got the head's job at Sara Bailey's school. Is that any help?'

'It certainly gives us a clearer picture Helen, thank you. As I said earlier I will need to get a statement from you, but that won't be for a day or two. I've got your number now so I'll fix something up and come and see you at your school after you finish so your husband, Graham, won't be around. I don't want to embarrass you.'

'As I said, he does know about what happened with me and Adam, but yes I'd feel better if you came to the school.'

'Well thank you again Helen and I'll be in touch.' Ending the call, Scarlett diverted her attention back to the forensics team, who were now by the edge of the canal – the three of them, standing side-by-side – staring into the murky waterway.

Fifty-one

'Have you got something?' Scarlett called out, yomping down the incline to the CSI team. There were now three yellow forensic pyramids on the ground by Adam Witton's BMW, each set beside a stained area of gravel.

One of the forensic officers turned and gave her a silent greeting as she joined them by the canal's edge. Scarlett studied the ripples. The greyness of the morning reflected in the water. 'Found something?' she asked again.

'Not sure,' mumbled the man, pulling down his face mask. 'Both the driver's seat and back seat of the BMW are covered in blood, and there are small areas of blood leading to here, together with scuff marks along the ground.'

'Is that what the markers are covering?'

The man nodded and pointed to a tiny stain, no bigger than a two pence piece, in front of them at the edge of the canal. 'And there's this small area of blood. We think someone went into the canal at this point here.'

'Jumped or fallen?'

The three forensic officers shrugged simultaneously. The man said, 'The amount of blood in the car and the drag marks would suggest that whoever came from that car would be in a pretty bad state.'

'You know this is linked to the Trish Scarr murder, two days ago? The pathologist who did her PM found skin under her fingernails. Could it mean she fought back more than we think?'

'Given the amount of blood, it would suggest she put up a hell of a fight. Like I said, the blood loss is significant.'

'But why blood in the front, as well as the back of the car?'

Another member of the CSI team removed their mask and turned to face Scarlett. She was a slim woman who looked to be in her late thirties. 'The patterns are completely different. The blood-staining in the driver's seat looks to be transfer stains – blood, which, more than likely has come from the blood-stained clothes they are wearing. The blood in the back is thicker – some of it congealed. That looks to have come from an area that has bled out. Totally different.'

Scarlett eyebrows narrowed, 'Meaning?'

The woman gave another shrug, 'This is merely supposition based on the information we've been given. Let's just say that Adam's driven here straight after the murder, with some kind of injury from his fight with the victim – let's just say to his head for now, given the different pattern on the front seat. The blood loss would have made him feel faint and so he got into the back seat to lie down, which is why the blood has pooled there.'

'And after a while he's got to thinking what he's just done, decided the game's up, dragged himself to the edge of the canal here and thrown himself in?' Scarlett interjected, looking down at the slate coloured water.

'That's one line of thinking. But the only way we're going to know for certain is by searching this canal,' answered the woman.'

Scarlett returned to the outer cordon and put in a call to Diane Harris, updating her about the blood-trail evidence and what it could mean, and requesting the attendance of the Marine Police Unit to search the waterway. The DCI told her she would put in the request immediately and to inform her the moment they had anything of significance, before ending the phone-call with a 'Well done.' Scarlett stuffed her BlackBerry back into her pocket and went to her car, checking the time. It would be at least an hour before the Marine Police Unit got to her – enough time to make a few notes in her journal while she waited.

Fifty-two

It took a lot less time for the Marine Police Unit to arrive than Scarlett had anticipated – the Sergeant who introduced his team said they had been about to go out on a training exercise when they had got the call, so their dinghy and kit was already loaded in the trailer. However, it was mid-afternoon by the time they were kitted-up and on the water because the Unit's van and trailer were too large for the cemetery's main gates and everything had to be manhandled down to the water's edge. It was frustrating.

Making a mental note of the time, Scarlett watched four neoprene-suited men lower themselves, and their diving gear, into their craft and gently push away from the bank. One started the outboard engine, steered the dinghy gently away in a straight line towards the centre of the canal, and then began circling steadily. It took a good ten minutes for two of the squad to equip themselves with air tanks and weight belts before signalling they were ready. They dropped backwards off the side of the dinghy, entering the oily water with a heavy splash that rocked their boat. For a second they bobbed about in a gentle swell, adjusting their masks and second-testing their breathing regulators, and then, giving a thumbs up to the boat crew, they disappeared into the murk. Although the canal was only about three metres deep, such was the poor quality of the water that she couldn't see anything of them below the surface, though she could follow their progress from the air bubbles breaking the light ebb.

A metre from where Scarlett was standing, the bubbles stopped in their tracks. Her heart picked up a beat.

Two minutes later a diver came to the surface. Easing up his mask and removing his mouth regulator, he said, 'We've found a body.'

**

It was another three-quarters of an hour before they brought the body up. The corpse was hauled up by rope, first to the dinghy's side and then carefully pulled on board. From where Scarlett was she couldn't make out if it was Adam Witton or not and she fought back her excitement. Five minutes later the boat was just below her but she still couldn't see if it was their suspect because the body was face down. Getting the cadaver up onto the towpath took cautious manoeuvring under the watchful instruction of the lead forensic officer. Finally, a quarter of an hour later, following vigilant handling, the Marine Unit had the body laid out on heavy plastic sheeting.

It was Adam Witton.

He was only wearing one shoe. The other must have come off when they dragged him up from the bottom of the canal. She scanned his body. His face was wax-white, the skin water-crinkled, and his dark hair matted with weed, as were his shirt and trousers.

Two of the CSI team nodded before stepping onto the sheeting, which crackled underfoot. While one fastened plastic bags onto Adam's hands the other took a series of photographs. Then they started their examination. One held and supported Witton's head as the other delicately parted strands of hair. Only thirty seconds after starting his probing, the lead forensic officer looked up at Scarlett. 'You need to get your SIO down here pronto. And the pathologist. This is not as we first thought.'

Fifty-three

At the cemetery gates Scarlett was pacing around like a hungry animal at a zoo. It had been well over an hour since she had called it in over the radio and there was still no sign of her DCI. She'd tried ringing Diane Harris but her mobile rang out until diverting to voicemail. She was about to call the incident room again when the DCI's car came speeding towards her. After screeching to a halt Diane Harris flung open the door.

'We've got a problem,' she shouted over the roof of her car, going to the boot and popping the lid.

Scarlett quickly joined her. 'What's the matter?'

Removing a Tyvek forensic suit from inside, Diane glanced sideways. 'Just before you radioed in, I'd just got the results back from the lab.' Slinging the all-in-one over her arm and picking out two over-shoe bootees, she slammed down the lid. 'Alice Witton's DNA is all over Trish's face and arms, and the skin under Trish's nails – Alice's.'

Scarlett took a sharp intake of breath. 'Alice killed Trish?'

Diane Harris nodded.

'Has she been arrested?'

'That's the problem. I sent George and Ella to pick her up once I got the phone call from the lab and they found Lucy unconscious in the kitchen. She'd been hit over the head with an empty wine bottle. We believe Alice heard your message on Lucy's radio. She's done a runner. I've got everyone out looking for her. Hayden's coordinating.'

'Good God! Is Lucy okay?'

'Nasty cut and concussion. She's at the hospital. Ella's with her.' Slipping off her jacket, the DCI opened the passenger door of her car, slung it onto the seat and started unravelling her forensic suit. 'Tell me what you've got.'

Scarlett said, 'Adam's body was found at the bottom of the canal. We thought at first he might have topped himself, but CSI have found a hole in the back of his head that you can get your fist inside. He's been whacked with something really heavy. The supervisor believes that given the state of the injury and the amount of blood on the back seat he would have been dead before he went in the water. I was going to tell you it's looking like he was murdered, but that's no surprise now. Especially given what you've just said about Alice. And given what you've just said, we know who killed him.'

'What about the Pathologist?'

'Still on his way.'

'Okay, let's have a look then, shall we?'

They set off at a march down the path.

Fifty-four

The DCI called everyone back shortly before 6 p.m. In the ensuing 30 minutes, the squad filtered in gradually, each asking the other what was happening. Everyone was puzzled.

Scarlett was one of the last back in the office. After the DCI had left she had remained with Adam Witton's body, waiting for the Pathologist. Niall Lynch had turned out, making her wait worthwhile: Niall was a charming Irishman in his late forties whom she'd met at many crime scenes. His gallows humour and macabre stories always kept her entertained no matter what the tragedy. He'd carried out a short but methodical examination of Adam Witton's body, confirming what CSI had already told her about cause of death – the head injury. A rectal test revealed Witton had been dead well over 24 hours. It would first thing tomorrow morning before the post-mortem – Niall was on his way to another body – someone hit by a train near South Ruislip underground, and waving his goodbye, he'd left her with the words, 'No rest for the wicked eh!' Scarlett had overseen the body being removed by the undertakers. She was alone by the time the black van had turned up – everyone had packed up and left. Once she had seen the two dour-faced undertaker's assistants off with Adam's body, she had left, calling into the hospital on her way back to base to check on how her new partner was doing. Lucy had been stitched up and bandaged and was still on a trolley waiting to see the doctor again; she'd been told to stay in overnight for observation because of concussion, but she didn't want to and was waiting to be re-assessed.

It was while Scarlett was at the hospital she got the DCI's call to come in. She bade Lucy cheerio, telling her that she would see her later and hurried back to the station. Before going into the office though she decided to put in a call to Tarn. It seemed unfair not to let him know what was going on, given that the DNA results pointed the finger of suspicion at Alice Witton for the murder of his wife: she would never forgive herself if he found it out from the news. He answered within seconds. She said, 'Tarn, it's me, I've got some news, but I can't talk long.'

'You've got Adam Witton.'

She gave a wry smile. She should have expected that. 'Well yes we have, but it's not happened the way we expected.' She outlined how they had found Adam's body in the canal and that an autopsy was being performed on his body tomorrow. Before he could butt in she said, 'But he didn't kill Trish.' Tarn went quiet and Scarlett guessed he was filtering everything, pulling his thoughts together.

After a few seconds he responded, 'Adam didn't kill Trish! Then who did?'

'His wife! Alice! We know because her DNA's all over Trish. We got the results back from the lab this lunchtime.' Pausing she continued, 'Look Tarn, I know there's a hundred-and-one things you want to ask me, but all I can tell you is there are a few complications, and we've got loads of things to follow up, which I can't go into at the moment. We've all just been called back for an emergency briefing so I should be getting an update on the state-of-play very shortly. Once I find out what's happening I promise I'll come back to you.' Before he could ask any further questions she hung up, turned off her mobile and headed for the incident room. She had just got herself a coffee from the machine down the hall and settled into her seat when Diane Harris and Hayden Taylor-Butler strode into the office, both wearing bleak looks.

Everyone stopped what they were doing. Scarlett set down her polystyrene cup of weak looking coffee. She'd already gone off the thought of drinking it.

'We have news. Good and bad.' Diane Harris addressed the squad. 'Following a search of Witton's home we believe we have the weapon that killed Adam. We've found a broken metal ornament in their refuse bin at the back of the house and it's got bloodstains on it. That's the good news.' She scanned the room.

'The bad news is that Alice Witton is dead. It looks like she's committed suicide. I got a phone call an hour ago from BTP. A woman jumped in front of a train just outside South Ruislip station at four-forty p.m. this afternoon. They've identified her from the photograph we circulated.' She paused again. 'Because of the state her body's in, we've got a DNA test to run as a matter of formality, but we're happy it is Alice Witton. I've spoken to Lucy at the hospital and she's confirmed the clothing she was wearing today and it fits with that on the body. And we've also got to do a DNA test on the ornament recovered from Witton's bin, but on the face of it that looks like the end of our investigation. Alice Witton killed Trish Scarr and then her husband. Sadly we'll never know exactly why, but we can all guess.' Placing her hands together she scanned the room, smiled and said, 'And mentioning Lucy - just to let everyone know, she's fine. Understandably she's got a bit of a headache, but I spoke to her a few minutes ago and she says she doesn't have to stay in tonight – they're releasing her as we speak.' She added, 'And now as is customary on these occasions, the first round is on me.'

Fifty-five

The Homicide and Serious Crime Unit should have been in celebratory mood, given that they had successfully solved two murders, but the atmosphere in the Old Bank pub, on Sutton High Street felt more like a wake. Scarlett was standing with Ella and George, sipping beer from a bottle and deliberating over the outcome of the investigation. Under normal circumstances, the fact they had their killer, albeit the killer was dead, should have been seen as a good result. But one of the victims was the wife of a good friend and colleague and that overshadowed everything. George had summed it up quite eloquently – 'Alice Witton didn't just have mental health issues, she also had betrayal issues, and she didn't just take it out on her husband.' The three of them had also come to the conclusion that it was probably Alice who was responsible for the damage to Helen Davis' car, though they would never know now.

For a brief moment, beer bottle pressed firmly to her lips, yet not drinking, Scarlett's thoughts drifted from their conversation. She thought about the impact this would have on Tarn and wondered if he would ever be able to pick up the pieces – especially thinking of his two young children, Heather and Dale and how they had been affected. Her musing was shattered by Ella, who nudged her arm and said, 'I forgot to tell you I saw James Green – at least I think it was him. He was a fair distance away from me, but it certainly looked like him.'

Ella's words yanked back her attention. 'Where?' she said sharply.

'On Tarn's street, the other day, when we were doing house-to-house. He was standing on the corner watching us.'

Ella's response triggered memories of Scarlett chasing the stranger she had seen taking a photograph of her on his phone. She told Ella and George about it.

'Bloody hell Scarlett, he is stalking you.'

'I know that. That's what I've been telling Taylor-Butler these past couple of weeks, but it's like banging my head on a brick wall talking to him about James Green.' She glanced over to where she had last seen the DI sitting. He was still at the same table holding court with Diane Harris. She turned back to George and Ella. 'He thinks I'm being a drama queen.'

'Do you want me to mention it?'

'Do you mind, Ella? Once we tidy up everything from this enquiry I want to bring it up with the gaffer. I'd like to catch James Green bang to rights, but the only way that's going to happen is if we target him. At the moment the boss won't sanction it, because TB's got her ear, but if you tell her you've seen him as well, she might go for it.'

Ella touched her arm, 'Sure I will. The guy's a creep.'

Scarlett thanked her, finished her beer and asked Ella and George if they wanted another. They did. She went to the bar, set down her empty bottle, and was about to order three drinks when a rapturous applause erupted behind her. She turned to see Lucy Summers, head bandaged, standing by the doorway and looking embarrassed. Diane Harris rose to greet her, planting a hand on her shoulder.

The DCI announced, 'This brave lady deserves a drink, but on doctor's orders it will be juice.'

A round of laughter followed another cycle of clapping as Diane Harris brought her into the room.

Breaking into a smile, Scarlett caught Lucy's attention with a wave, pointed to her empty bottle and ordered her a Coke.

***

After three bottles Scarlett decided she'd had enough – she wasn't in the mood to party. Following her second drink she had texted Alex because she fancied his company tonight but he had texted her back that he was away from home for a couple of days. That had only added to her morose mood. Setting down her empty bottle she made an excuse that she was knackered, told Ella and George she wanted an early night and left the pub. The street was filled with a moisture laden veil of mist that blurred anything beyond fifty yards. The temperature had also dropped and she shuddered, pulled on her leather jacket and hitched up the collar. For a moment, she stood with her back to the pub looking around. There was some traffic passing but it was light. In the couple of seconds she had been there, her thoughts returned again to James Green. Images of him replayed in her mind, triggered by Ella's mention of him earlier. Another involuntary shake travelled through her, but this time it wasn't the cold. Casting another look around, trying her best to pierce the fine grey shroud blocking her view, her heart began to palpitate. She couldn't help but wonder if he was hiding out there, watching her right now.

Fifty-six

A ringing noise wrenched Scarlett out of a deep sleep. In a state of confusion she blinked. Darkness surrounded her. The ringing was coming from her BlackBerry. Work! Quickly rolling over she snatched up her phone while getting a look of her bedside clock. The green luminous numbers told her it was 03:28. This had to be urgent. Levering herself up onto one arm she answered 'Hello.' Her voice caught in her throat. She cleared it and was about to speak again when a man's voice called her name. It only took her a split-second to identify it. Ryan Anderson – Ella's boyfriend. He sounded worried.

'Ryan! What's up?'

'Is Ella with you, Scarlett?'

'Ella?'

'Yes Ella. She said she was going out to meet you. Where are you?'

'In bed – where I should be. It's almost half-three in the morning. What do you mean Ella said she was going out to meet me?'

'Jesus.'

She caught the anxiety in his tone. 'Ryan, what's the matter?'

'Ella said she was going out to meet you. Something to do with our burglary.'

What Ryan had just said didn't make any sense. She wondered if she was still woolly from her deep sleep. 'I'm not with you, Ryan. The last time I spoke to Ella was in the pub. All the team went for a drink after briefing. I left early. She was with George when I left.'

'And you haven't been called out over our break-in?'

Now Scarlett was really confused. 'Ryan, I don't know what you're talking about.'

'Christ, Scarlett. I think Ella's in danger.'

Scarlett pushed herself up. 'What do you mean?'

'Ella took a call just after midnight. She said it was from communications – you were requesting she join you and it was to do with our burglary. She went out almost three hours ago and I've tried ringing her but she's not answering.'

Ryan's voice had risen several notches. She caught his sense of panic. 'Did she say where I was supposed to be meeting her?'

'No, she said she'd probably be a couple of hours and if she was going to be any longer she'd text. As I've said, that was almost three hours ago now.'

'Is she in her own car?'

'Yeah.'

'Listen Ryan, get back onto comms and see if they can get a trace on Ella's phone and give them her reg number. I'm going to call the gaffer and go to the nick. You stay put and I'll be in touch.' She added, 'I'm sure there's some simple explanation for this Ryan.' As she ended the call, she thought about what she'd just said. They were the words you said on autopilot – words you were trained to deliver when you were trying to reassure. Even though she'd said them, she knew Ryan wouldn't be reassured. Both he and she knew something wasn't right.

***

Scarlett tore into work on her bike. As soon as she got into the incident room she contacted Communications and spoke with the duty Inspector. No one from his department had made a call to Ella that evening, and he'd put out a nationwide alert for sightings of Ella's car and a track on her phone. The Inspector told Scarlett Ella's phone was not responding and he was requesting a GPS coordinate for its last known location. Everything was being cranked up to find her.

Ten minutes later, Diane Harris walked in asking for an update, which Scarlett gave. She had just finished when Hayden Taylor-Butler strode in too. Although Scarlett didn't have much time for the DI she was grateful for him being there.

Checking her notes from Scarlett's briefing Diane Harris rang Ryan Anderson and got him to repeat what he'd earlier told Scarlett, checking the last time he had seen Ella. Ending the call with, 'We're doing everything we can to find Ella,' she turned to face Scarlett and Hayden, looking concerned. 'This is not looking good,' she said grimly. 'I'm setting up an incident immediately. The nearest nick to Ella's place is Camberwell. I'm going to send a couple of detectives round there – not that I don't believe what Ryan's telling us but I need to cover all bases.' To Scarlett she said, 'Any thoughts? You know Ella better than me.'

'James Green,' Scarlett answered.

Hayden threw her a dagger's look.

Scarlett rounded on him. 'Look I know you think I'm fixated with him, and yes I probably am, but the things he's been up to since his release have fuelled that fixation.' She heaved a frustrated sigh and added, 'You asked me my thoughts and I've given you an answer.' She repeated what Ella had told her earlier that evening about seeing Green near Tarn's house three days ago. 'I saw him as well. In fact, I chased him but lost him in one of the gardens.' Following a short pause, she continued, 'I've been giving this some thought since I got here. Remember the incident at the So Bar?'

Both Diane Harris and Hayden Taylor-Butler nodded.

'That was Ella's engagement do. I thought at the time when I confronted him that he was there stalking me – but what if he wasn't? I braced him up as you know and he left, and that same night Ella and Ryan's flat was broken into. She told me nothing had been stolen. She said her BlackBerry and iPad were on the side but they hadn't been touched. She thought they had disturbed whoever had broken in and they'd fled before they had time to take anything.' Scarlett looked from DCI to DI. 'But what if the person who broke in wasn't just your average burglar? What if nothing had been taken, because they had actually broken into Ella and Ryan's flat to access her work phone? It wouldn't be too hard to programme in a number and index it as Communications, would it?' Pausing again she said, 'All along I've been thinking James Green was stalking me, but he wasn't. It was Ella! She was the one who posed as a student to trap him. That's how we caught him.' She locked eyes with her DCI. 'This is Green getting his revenge.'

'Bloody hell Scarlett, at this stage I'd listen to any ideas or thoughts, no matter how wild, but I have to say what you're telling me does make sense.' Taking a deep breath, DCI Harris stroked her chin and looked up to the ceiling for a few seconds. 'Right, we've got uniform out there looking for her car and comms trying to get a lock on her phone. I want you, Hayden, to start coordinating things, and you, Scarlett, to give me everything you know about James Green, ready for when the team come in.' Diane Harris was writing another note when the phone on Scarlett's desk started ringing. Everyone turned and stared at it.

Fifty-seven

The call was from the Communication Department: Ella's car had been found abandoned at a derelict industrial estate at Greenwich.

Scarlett, Diane Harris, and Hayden Taylor-Butler dropped what they were doing and raced over there in the DCI's car. By the time they arrived the pot-holed entranceway had been cordoned off and two uniform officers were stopping anyone from entering.

Thirty yards ahead Scarlett spotted Ella's white Seat car parked next to a large graffiti-covered concrete warehouse. She threw open her door, making ready to leave before Diane Harris had even stopped the car.

The DCI called her back. 'Suit up Scarlett. I understand your urgency, but we still do this by the book.' She turned into the kerb and braked. 'I've got spares in the back.'

Removing their overcoats and dropping them into the boot, Scarlett, Diane and Hayden zipped themselves into forensic suits, pulling up the hoods as they strode over to the cordon.

'Was DC Bloom's car the only one here when you arrived?' Diane Harris asked the two PCs standing by the first line of blue and white tape. She showed them her identification, pulling the lanyard over her head.

'Yes boss.' The officer with the crime-scene logbook answered. He made a note of Diane Harris's name.

'Any sign of her?'

The PC shook his head.

'Anything left in her car?'

'Not as far as I know.'

'And no one around?'

The PC shook his head again. 'Just her car there.'

'Who found it?'

'I don't know exactly boss. Everyone else has gone into the site to carry out a search just in case she's in there. My Sergeant's in there, she'll know.'

'And was the driver's door open like that?' Diane pointed to Ella's car.

The PC nodded, following the line of the DCI's outstretched arm. 'I understand there's some blood just by it. It's not much. CSI have been requested.'

Scarlett's stomach lurched and a shiver ran up her spine. *Blood!* For a moment she stared at Ella's abandoned car and then gathered her thoughts and started scouring the area. The sky was just registering daylight, a pale orange glow smudging the horizon. The derelict industrial estate, mainly consisting of concrete and brick warehouses, looked pretty substantial and she guessed that carrying out a thorough search of every building was going to take most of the day. Somehow though, she knew they were not going to find Ella here. It was James Green's flat they should be heading to.

'And the driver's side tyre's flat. Probably a puncture. There are nails all over the road. Looks like they've been put there recently. They're new.'

The Officer's comment caught Scarlett's attention. This has been very cleverly planned, she thought.

Suited up, the three of them made their way towards Ella's car to get a better look. Several yards from it they stopped and began looking around. Scarlett scanned the empty weed-infested road, giving a cursory glance to the boarded up, graffiti clad warehouses lining the perimeter, before her gaze returned to Ella's car. She saw the blood the PC had mentioned. At least she thought it was blood. In this half-light she couldn't be sure – the small puddle glistened, so it was reasonably fresh. She could also make out scrape marks around it. It looked like there had been a scuffle. *Ella had fought back? Maybe. Hopefully.* If she had, that might give them some forensic evidence to rest their hopes on. She started to shake. *Shock!* Something she hadn't experienced in a while. It had hit her after the police came to tell her that her parents were dead, and on the morning Aunt Hanna died in the hospice when she had sat with her all night. Not even after the London bombings, when one of the victims had died in her arms, did she suffer from shock, yet now she was shaking like a leaf. She looked up to the sky. Strands of blue had started break through the bank of grey clouds.

'Scarlett!'

Diane Harris's sharp cry brought her back to the present.

'I was just saying Scarlett, I don't think we can do anything else here for now. CSI are on their way and there's the search of the buildings to be done. You and I will be better served getting back to the station and organising the team.'

Fifty-eight

DI Taylor-Butler remained at the scene to liaise with CSI and co-ordinate a thorough search of the empty units and lock-ups, while Scarlett and DCI Harris returned to the office. They got back shortly before 8 a.m. The majority of the team were in and the moment the pair entered the office they were firing questions at them about Ella: word had already got out.

Diane Harris raised a hand, 'Listen guys, I've just got to make a few quick phone calls to let Gold Command know what's happening, then I'll do briefing. Get yourself a drink and a quick snack, because it's going to be a very long day.'

She turned and left, leaving Scarlett to fend off the barrage of questions from her worried colleagues.

***

By eight-thirty, briefing was under way. The DCI took up her place by the incident board, though it was still full of photographs and information from the Trish Scarr murder – they hadn't had time to clear it. A silent Homicide Squad waited for news about their fellow worker.

Diane Harris began, 'Morning everyone, I'm going to open up by saying this is one of the most daunting briefings I have ever had to give and I hope I will never have to repeat it.' She took a breath, 'According to Ella's partner, Ryan Anderson, who I think most of you know is a detective at Brixton, Ella took a call around midnight last night, on her work phone, purportedly from Communications, to the effect that Scarlett, here, had requested she join her in relation to the burglary they had at their flat ten days ago.' After a pause, she said, 'We know Scarlett never made a call and Communications never made any such call to Ella. At just after two-thirty this morning Ryan began ringing Ella's phone because he was concerned she hadn't called to update him about what was happening. He said he rang her phone six times. The first four times it rang until it went through to her voicemail. The last two times it went straight to voicemail. Then he rang Scarlett, who told him she had made no such call and that was when I was contacted.' She halted again, 'Shortly before 6.30 this morning, uniform found her car abandoned at an old industrial site at Greenwich. The driver's side front tyre had suffered a puncture, caused by a nail. Hayden is at the scene and he has just updated me with that information. We found dozens of them scattered all over the road not far from her car, which makes me believe that this was pre-planned. There is no sign of Ella. We have carried out a cursory search of the area, and we are now conducting a more thorough search of all the buildings and grounds around that site.' For a third time she broke off, taking in a deep breath. 'What is disturbing is that we have found blood by the driver's side of her car and signs of a scuffle. It is not a lot of blood, but nevertheless it is blood, so we think she might be injured.' Tight-lipped, she added, 'While I am ruling nothing in or out, I am currently treating Ella's disappearance as abduction and so the priority right now is to trace her. While we haven't found her phone, and we know it's switched off, or the battery has been taken out, we can access her phone record, so I've just put in an urgent request to the Tech Team to see if they can trace and locate the number that called her at just after midnight.' Surveying the room, she said, 'The clock is ticking on this, everyone. We have no idea what has happened to Ella, and until we get access to her phone calls, we have no clear leads, but we do have supposition.' To Scarlett, she said, 'Will you tell everyone what you told me earlier about your thoughts on James Green?'

Fifty-nine

In the dim light, fastened to a chair, Ella Bloom struggled against her bonds. The plastic ties were chafing her wrists, hurting her, but that was nothing to the pain to her head. The injury from the blow that had knocked her unconscious had stopped bleeding but she could feel the crusted blood on her cheeks as she tried desperately to get free. She tried to scream again but the duct tape across her mouth reduced it to a stifled moan. Within seconds she was drained and she slumped back and started to cry. It was her fifth attempt at trying to break free since she had woken and she was determined not to give in. She was still trying to fathom out why she was here – tied up. The last thing she could remember was cursing her flat tyre. That's when she'd been clobbered from behind. She had heard footsteps but hadn't had time to turn around before she was hit. The sharp blow and flashing stars were a distant memory now.

The sound of a door opening behind her made her jump. For a few seconds light flooded in and she saw a sparsely furnished room with a video camera on a tripod in the right-hand corner. As the door closed and the light disappeared, panic surged through her. *Terrorists!* Months ago, they had been briefed about home-grown Jihadists planning to abduct a member of the police or armed services. A soldier had already been murdered – almost beheaded – not too far away. *Fuck!* She began to shake as a dark figure brushed past and stood before her. Whoever was standing in front was just a silhouette. The person was slim and they were wearing a hoodie. She tried to shout through her gag but her lips hardly parted and it came out as an indecipherable cry.

Whoever it was sniggered. Ella got the impression it was a man from the deep tone. He bent towards her and fear gripped. She tried to flinch away but it was impossible. Not just her wrists and hands were tied but her middle was also taped to the chair. She fought to suppress a sob as he as he pressed his face ever closer. She suddenly recognised her captor. James Green! Even in the low light she could see a maniacal smile plastered across his face. She was terrified.

'You forced me to do this you know.' The words came slow and soft but were nevertheless menacing. 'This is all your fault. Yours and Detective Macey's.'

A sharp movement flashed and she looked down at something long and thin he was tapping in his hand. She caught a diffused glint along its shaft. It looked like metal. It reminded her of a small section of scaffolding.

He swung it towards her, pushing it to her chest, catching her breast bone. It stung for a second. He rested the pole there for a brief moment and then started to tease it down until it came to her lap where he let the end rest. His eyes fixed hers. They were black and feral. Suddenly she was cold and started to shiver. Thoughts of Ryan jumped inside her head: their weekend in Paris: Their plans for the wedding: Dad walking her down the aisle. Would she ever see them again? She didn't want to die. She started crying.

He slowly pushed the steel rod into her genital area. 'By the time I've finished, you're going to be begging me to kill you,' he said quietly.

Sixty

DCI Harris had tasked Scarlett with providing background information about James Green in readiness for the next briefing. So, reluctant to confess she already had copious notes about him from the files she'd smuggled home, she kept her head down, pretending to be busy, and then an hour later sneaked out the earlier written record from her locked bottom drawer. The one thing she had added were her thoughts that Green's flat at Twickenham was only a transit address, based upon the photographic evidence, and her deliberation with Alex – though she left out the bit about Alex viewing the CSI photos. Everyone was busy – making phone calls or working on their computers – so she made herself a coffee and returned to her desk. The incident board had been cleared of the Trish Scarr investigation and now an A4 photograph of Ella was posted upon it. The image was one taken five years earlier, when she was in uniform, but she hadn't changed much. For a moment Scarlett stared at it. She thought about what James Green had done to his victims and she shuddered. She hoped to God they would find Ella before he did anything to her. Looking away from Ella's photo, Scarlett stood. She'd nail the bastard this time!

She grabbed her paperwork, shuffled it together and headed off to see the DCI.

***

Scarlett juggled with the wheel and a bottle of water, opening the top with her teeth and taking a sip. She handed it back to George Martin in the passenger seat.

'So what is it we're doing exactly?' George asked, screwing the lid back on the bottle and placing it in the doorwell.

George was her partner for the day: Lucy was office-bound until the stitches came out of her head wound, and Tarn, although re-instated, had taken a week off to prepare for his wife's funeral and be with his family. She answered, 'A quick recce of James Green's place. I know there's nothing to prove he's abducted Ella, and nothing's come yet from the crime scene, but the minute we have something we'll be ready to strike. I told the DCI I think Green has another place, somewhere other than his flat and she's given me permission to make some discreet enquiries.'

George's bushy eyebrows knitted together, 'And what exactly does discreet mean? I've never known you be discreet.'

Scarlett shot him a quick look, 'George Martin, how could you?'

'Only speaking the truth.'

She laughed. 'Well, what I thought is, we'll get our bearings at his flat is – it's five months since I was last there – and make a few enquiries with his neighbours to see if anyone's seen him recently. If we get anything I've promised Diane Harris I'll give her a bell and wait for instructions.'

'That seems discreet enough for me.'

'Glad you approve Detective.' Smiling, Scarlett indicated right and pulled across the lane into the junction: They were only a minute away from James Green's place.

***

Scarlett parked two streets away and, with George backing her up, made the rest of the way there on foot. Green's one-bedroom flat was on the first floor of a long red-brick building of one- and two-bedroom apartments, just a stone's-throw from St. Margaret's railway station. Entrance to the complex was gained by double doors into a foyer. An electronic keypad provided security and Scarlett had forgotten the code since her last visit. She was just considering her best options for gaining access without alerting Green if he was at home, when one of the doors opened and out came a plump, grey-haired, woman, in her late sixties, or early seventies. Head down, she was struggling with a shopping trolley. Its wheel had caught on the door, and she was trying to tug it free. Scarlett took hold of the door and held it, allowing the woman to release her trolley.

'Thank you dear,' she said, looking up at Scarlett.

She looked familiar. Smiling, Scarlett said, 'Do you know a James Green who lives here?'

The elderly woman's eyes narrowed for a second, then lit up. She pointed at Scarlett's hair. 'You're that Detective who was here when he was locked up, aren't you? The papers said he'd raped them students.'

Scarlett's smile widened. It was Green's next-door neighbour. During their enquiries, after he had been arrested, she said she had seen him burning things in an old oil drum at the rear of the flats. Thanks to her help they had found charred remnants of clothing, though sadly, nothing of evidential value. 'You remembered.'

'This body may be old but my mind's still sharp. Nothing much gets past me. How come you let him out? Did he get off at court?'

Scarlett shook her head. She didn't want to spend the next ten minutes trying to explain things. She replied, 'It's a long story.'

The lady straightened her shopping trolley, tapping one wheel with her foot. 'Well if you're here to see him, you'll have a long wait.'

'A long wait?'

'I think you'll find he's done a moonlight.'

'Why's that then?'

'Only seen him twice since he came out. They painted his door while he was inside. Kids! Sprayed it. I saw him cleaning it off the day he got out, but he only stayed there the one night, I think. I haven't heard him moving about, like I normally do. Last time I saw him was about a week ago. I was just down the shops – where I'm going now – and I saw him coming out of the supermarket with some flowers. He was carrying a suitcase. Looked like he was going somewhere. He never saw me.'

The thought of James Green with flowers and a suitcase was intriguing. 'You're sure it was James?'

The woman pulled a face and appeared put out, 'Sure I'm sure. I only need glasses for reading, not distances.'

'I'm sorry. I was just making absolutely certain.'

'Why? Has he raped someone else?'

Scarlett's mouth tightened. *I hope not!* She answered with the first thing that came into her head, 'No, we just need to check something back with him. You said he had some flowers. Does he have a girlfriend?'

'Not that I know of. They were for his mum. He always bought her a bunch when he visited her.'

'His mum!' Scarlett remembered asking him about his parents when he was in custody. He told her they were both dead. 'Do you know where she lives?'

'I think she's in a home, dear. Dementia, or something like that. I remember him telling me once.'

'Do you know which home she's in?'

She shook her head. 'I never asked, but I think it's not too far away. He used to go on his bike.'

'You don't know her name by any chance, do you?'

For a moment the lady looked skywards, concentrating. She murmured, 'It's something to do with a film. Now what was she called?' After a few more seconds of looking studious she smiled, 'Dorothy. That's it. Dorothy. As in *The Wizard of Oz*. I knew it was something to do with a film I'd seen.'

'Thank you.'

'Have I been some help to you dear?'

Scarlett stroked her arm. 'You've been more than helpful.'

'Good. Now, as much as I'd like to, I can't stand here chatting all day. I said I'd meet Emily at eleven for coffee.' With that the woman set off, almost at a trot, pulling her shopping trolley behind her.

Scarlett watched her go and said, 'I hope I'm as sprightly when I'm her age.' To George she added, 'Come on. Now we're here, let's have a quick look around.'

Sixty-one

Scarlett and George took the stairs to the first floor. As they neared James Green's flat they could see the blurred remains of the spray-can art the neighbour had spoken of. Across his black door, the word RAPIST, in silver, was still evident.

Good, Scarlett thought. She put an ear to the door and listened for the best part of thirty seconds. She tried the handle. It gave a fraction but was locked. Glancing at the Yale lock, she said softly, 'Well, shall we take a look?'

'Take a look?' whispered back George.

'Yes, you heard the neighbour. He's not here. What did she say – done a moonlight.'

'And how are we going to get in, it's locked?'

'It's only a Yale lock. Pretty flimsy. A little push and we'll be in.'

'And how are we going to cover forcing an entry?'

'You've seen the graffiti the kids have done. We'll just say we found it busted open.'

George rolled his eyes, 'Christ, Scarlett, I thought you said discreet.'

She tapped her nose, 'Ways and means George. Ways and means. Right, big man, gloves on and get your shoulder on that door.'

Shaking his head, he pulled on latex gloves from his jacket pocket, grabbed the handle and launched his shoulder at the door. There was a sharp crack but it held.

Scarlett held up her gloved hand, looked up and down the hallway and listened a second. Silence. She gave George the nod and he repeated his action. This time the door gave way and he almost fell inside. Holding onto the handle saved him from falling.

Scarlett tapped him on the shoulder. 'Well done.' She gave another look along the corridor before pushing George further inside and stepping into James Green's hallway. As she shut the door behind them she glanced at the lock and said quietly, 'You've hardly damaged it at all. We'll be able to screw that up easily. No one will be any the wiser. '

Scarlett remembered the layout from her last visit. To the right was the kitchen and lounge and at the far end of the hall was the bedroom and bathroom. For a moment she stood, listening. She got a strong whiff of disinfectant. Green must have done a thorough cleaning job before he left, she thought, and wondered what he was covering up. Pushing open the kitchen door she stepped inside. It was exactly the same as her last visit. The sides were clear. She remembered the crime scene photographs and the comments Alex had made about checking the cupboards for signs the place was lived in. In one wall cupboard, she found a couple of mugs and a few plates. The rest were empty. She opened the base unit doors. There were a few tins of food in one of them, but not enough for more than a couple of days. The sink unit contained a single pan, some cleaning materials and a couple of towels. There was a small fridge freezer, but it was empty and she could tell from the smell that it had been bleached clean.

With George bringing up the rear she went on to the lounge. Here was an old two-seater sofa, a chair, a wooden sideboard from the seventies and a large TV on top of a unit. There was no fireplace, just a wall mounted electric fire. On the floor was a cheap light brown carpet. On the walls were cheap prints of a vase of flowers, above the fire, and an autumn woodland scene above the sideboard. There were no family photographs or anything personal. It confirmed what Alex had said about this being merely a place for Green to get his head down from time to time.

They left the lounge and walked down the hallway to the bedroom. Even before she opened the door she knew from her last visit that all she was likely to see was a made up double bed, a bedside cabinet and a dark-wood double wardrobe. She pushed the door open. The room was gloomy, curtains closed. She went to the window and drew one aside to let in the light. As she turned back to look around the room her eyes fastened onto the large black writing on the wall above the bed headboard.

George had also seen it.

She read it twice before looking at George.

'What the fuck does that mean?' George asked.

She read it again.

WILL YOU PAY?
WHEN?
I DO NOT KNOW?
Have you worked it out yet Detective Macey?

She was sure she'd seen the writing before.

Sixty-two

Scarlett took a photo of the message with her phone; she would have to call this in. For a couple of seconds, she ran through things in her head. This was an important find. James Green was taunting her with some kind of puzzle, though she couldn't think what it meant. The issue however, was not about finding it, but how they had found it. They had made an illegal entry and if that was revealed, the discovery would be compromised. She had no other option but to lie. *It's only a little white lie!* So, after agreeing the story with George, she rang Diane Harris. She repeated what Green's neighbour had said, said they had found the door to his flat insecure and investigated, finding the message. 'He intended for me to find this,' she said. Diane Harris asked about the state of the flat and whether she needed CSI and Scarlett knew she'd been convincing. She took a sharp breath, 'No point. He's cleaned it from top to bottom. There's nothing here. Not even his clothes. It's as I thought, this is somewhere he put his head down from time to time. On the face of it, he made it look like he lived here. He's led us on a wild goose chase right from day one. I'm even more convinced, seeing this message, that he's got Ella.' She repeated the neighbour's comments about Green's mother, adding, 'He told me his parents were dead. James Green is just one big lie. I'm not even convinced that's his real name. I'm going to make a few more enquiries with the other neighbours and see if anyone else knows anything of his mum. I'm sure that if we find her, we'll find him. We'll be a couple of hours max and then come back to the office. Even if I find out where his mum is, I'll come back to the office first before doing anything.' Scarlett ended the call and turned to George. 'Come on big man, we've got some doors to knock on.'

***

Scarlett and George got back to the station shortly before lunch time. As she strode across the yard she got an incoming text on her personal mobile. It was Tarn, asking her if she could talk. She guessed he had heard about Ella. Probably seen it on the news. She told George to go ahead – that she would follow shortly – and rang him.

'Hi Tarn, are you okay?' She kept her tone low-key. The last thing she wanted was to sound cheerful given his tragedy.

'So, so. Not sleeping good. Went round to Trish's parents last night. They've been looking after Heather and Dale. It was the first time I've been able to see them since it happened.'

'And how did it go?'

'We all shed a few tears.'

Scarlett felt a lump in her throat and swallowed. 'That's understandable. How are the kids?'

'Heather's had a bad time of it. She misses her mum. But Dale doesn't seem to understand. Just keeps asking if mummy's gone to heaven.'

On that last sentence Tarn's voice started to crack. Her eyes began to well up. This was heart-breaking. Fighting her own emotion, she answered, 'He's probably too young. That might be a good thing.'

Tarn didn't immediately respond. There was a moment of uneasy silence and then he said, 'I've seen it on the news about Ella. They're saying it's abduction, with all kinds of speculation. I thought I'd give you a ring. See what's happened?'

She told him about the fake phone call that had lured Ella from her home and how her car had been found abandoned near the derelict industrial estate. 'To be honest we haven't got a clue what's happened to Ella. We've got everyone out trying to find her, but we haven't found anything that might point out where she is, or what's happened to her. I personally think it's something to do with all the stalking business by James Green and he's our main suspect at the moment.'

'I rang you to say if you needed any extra hands down there I'm willing to come in.'

Scarlett gulped, 'That's a lovely gesture Tarn, but everyone and his grandmother are involved in looking for her and I think you've got enough on your plate at the moment. Don't you?'

'Yes I guess so, but the offer's there if you need me.'

'Thank you, Tarn. I'll pass on your message.' Following an uncomfortable pause, she said, 'I'm sure the team will be in touch over the next few days and I'll ring you the moment we get something positive on Ella.'

'Thanks Scarlett.'

Just as she was about to say, 'look after yourself,' and end the call, Tarn said, 'I just wanted to say, as well, that Trish's funeral is next Tuesday. I haven't sorted all the details yet, but her mum and dad want a church service. I think it'll be where we got married.'

'I'll be there Tarn. Just let me know once you've got things sorted.' A tear ran down her cheek as she finished the call.

Sixty-three

By mid-afternoon, Scarlett had developed the mother of all headaches. She'd been on the go for twelve hours and was fast burning up her reserves. For the past twenty minutes she had reacquainted herself with James Green's antecedents and it hadn't taken her long to realise that there was very little that would help track him down. At the time of recording them she hadn't given it much thought, accepting what he had told her without question – now she was cursing herself for her slackness. In future she would probe more, she told herself, pushing his record to one side in frustration. Her vision had narrowed in the last few minutes and she was beginning to feel sick. She lifted her head to stare at the incident board. Ella's pretty face dominated the white space. Except for the timeline, highlighting the instance of her leaving her flat and pin-pointing the moment of finding her abandoned car, that's all they had by way of information. They were no nearer to finding her. Ella's BlackBerry was still off-line and its last point of contact was the industrial estate. Her car had been recovered and was currently drying out in a forensic garage awaiting examination, and the search of the old business site had just finished without any trace of her. Things were not looking good. Some of the team were currently going through footage from road-side cameras located between her flat and the industrial estate, to see if anyone had been following her car, but it was early days. The DCI had put up James Green's photograph, and written beneath it 'Suspect,' even though there wasn't a shred of evidence to support that notion. Though there were questions he needed to answer, specifically why he was at the So Bar, and on Tarn's street, when

Ella was doing house-to-house following Trish's murder. Diane Harris had tasked CSI with re-visiting Ella and Ryan's flat to carry out a more in-depth examination, in case anything had been missed after their break-in. There was nothing to suggest Green had carried out that burglary, nevertheless, he needed to be questioned about it: Scarlett's suspicions, with her reasoning behind it, needed answers. And then there was the message on Green's bedroom wall. It had been discussed at length, but its significance and meaning eluded them. Scarlett had told the squad she thought there were similarities in the handwriting style with that of something she had received anonymously a week ago and she produced the handwritten envelope, note and old coin from her drawer. It had now become an important piece of evidence. She also told the team about the bag of fruit she had received prior to the coin, and that provoked more debate, which drew no conclusion. The only conclusion the team came to – it was all part of a cat-and-mouse game James Green was playing, and while the main crux of their enquiries was the urgent need to find Ella, the other was tracing him. Scarlett turned her attention to Green's mug-shot, studying his features. With his waxed and ruffled straw-coloured hair, baby-blue eyes and strong jaw-line, given any other circumstances, she might have called him handsome. He'd been described as having the face of an angel. But since the suicide of Claudette Jackson, she thought of him as the Angel of Death.

Dragging her gaze away from Green's photograph, Scarlett launched into action, snatching up her desk phone. She'd suddenly remembered a contact in housing who might be able to help them find Green. She also had a number of nursing homes to call in the hope of finding Dorothy, his mother. There was still a lot of work to do before she called it a day.

***

As she climbed off her bike, Scarlett realised that she could remember very little of her drive home. The past thirty-five minutes had been a blur. She had done eighteen hours straight through and was exhausted. Unlocking the door and closing it behind her, she dragged her weary body out of her biking leathers and boots, and wandered into the kitchen, where she poured herself a glass of chilled water from the fridge and made her way upstairs. Drinking half of the water, she set the glass down on her dressing table, undressed, headed to the bathroom and climbed into the shower. Normally the warm water would have rejuvenated her, but not tonight. She was mentally and physically shattered, and all she wanted to do was curl up into a ball and sleep. She dried herself quickly, finished her glass of water, set her phone alarm for the morning and dropped down onto the bed. As she collapsed into her pillows and pulled over the duvet she hoped that nightmares about Ella weren't going to invade her already overtaxed brain.

Sixty-four

Scarlett could hear a ringing noise in her dream, until her brain told her it was her phone and she snapped awake. It was dark and it took her a few seconds to adjust. Her phone was still ringing and she picked it up, looking at the bedside clock as she answered. 05.31. There was something deja vu about this. She knew it was something important again.

'Sorry about this Scarlett.' It was Diane Harris. 'Ella's been found.'

There was nothing upbeat in the way the DCI delivered the message so she knew this was going to be bad news. 'It's not good, is it?'

'I'm afraid not Scarlett. She's been found dead in Richmond Park. I've just received the call, so I know very little at the moment, other than she's definitely been murdered. I tried to ring the duty Inspector who's at the scene, but I can't get hold of him, and I know it's not too far away from you, so I'm asking if you don't mind going down there to liaise with him and hold the fort until I get there. I know how close you were to Ella so I can understand if you don't want to. I can turn out Hayden instead.'

'No that's okay. It's literally five minutes' drive for me. I'll get myself sorted quickly and get down there.'

'Great. She was found by the Park Police. I'm guessing they'll be there as well. Get as much as you can, and call out who you need to call out. I should be with you within the hour.'

'No problem, boss.'

'And Scarlett…I'm sorry about this.'

***

The outer cordon was already in place by the time Scarlett got to Richmond Gate, her nearest entrance to the park, and a member of the Park Police was standing guard. She showed him her identification, informed him that her boss was on her way, and took the right-hand fork to Pembroke Lodge Gardens, where she parked her Triumph. Removing her helmet, she pulled on her all-in-one Tyvek suit and entered the Cafeteria grounds. It had been a good six months since she'd last been here, but the park had been a regular haunt through the years of living with her aunt and she knew her way around. A Met Officer acknowledged Scarlett with a nod and solemnly told her the body was on King Henry Eighth's Mound. Scarlett thanked her and made her way through the decorative grounds, onto the path that took her to the Mound. She soon came to the inner cordon. Here were another PC and the Inspector Diane Harris had mentioned during her phone call. He greeted her with, 'It's not a pretty sight I'm afraid. Was she a colleague?'

Scarlett nodded. How surreal – ten days ago they were celebrating Ella's engagement, Ella talking wedding plans, and now she was dead. *Life is so fucking cruel!* Shaking away the thought, she switched back into work mode. 'Have SOCO been contacted?'

'Requested half an hour ago,' replied the Inspector. 'The Pathologist has been contacted as well.'

'What time was she found?'

'Just before five. One of the Park Police guys found her on his rounds. He's ex-Met. Retired. His name's Rod Jones. He'd seen it on the news about DC Bloom going missing and recognised her immediately. He's currently going around the grounds with one of my team to see if they can see anyone.'

Scarlett made a mental note of the name. It might be some time before she got to speak with him: the grounds covered 2,500 acres, made up of many wooded areas, ponds, a golf course and children's play areas; it wasn't an easy place to search. Nodding she said, 'When he turns up can you tell him I need to speak with him. Oh, and my gaffer's on her way, it's the DCI you spoke with earlier. When she arrives, can you tell her where I am?' Ducking beneath the blue and white ribbon, Scarlett began her ascent to the top of the mound. The first fifty metres were overlooked by tall bushes and trees, but once free of those she stepped into a clearing, which gave her a spectacular panoramic view, down the vale, and across East Sheen Common to Richmond and Sheen, and where, at eye level, she watched green parrots swoop between the treetops. This morning, a fine mist drifted across the Common. She stopped for a second, taking in the beautiful view and trying not to think about what horrific sight lay ahead. After her short breather, she passed the last of the clipped hedgerows that lined the footpath, and stepped onto the top of the mound where the observation point was.

Ella's body lay a few yards away, just in front of bushes with a keyhole view to St. Paul's Cathedral. The sight of her friend, spread-eagled and naked, made her gasp out loud and she went light-headed. Thankfully she was next to the metal railings and she reached out and grabbed them. Controlling her breathing, steadying and calming herself, she released her grip and edged closer. It looked as if Ella had been dead some time. She had always been pale, but now Scarlett could see veins and blotches through the porcelain looking skin. What really grabbed her attention though was the damage to her genital area, the metal pole protruding from her vagina. The brutality did not end there: Ella's beautiful head had been severed from her body. Dropping to her knees, Scarlett screwed her eyes shut and covered her face with her hands. This was just too much to take in.

Sixty-five

The sound of squawking and shrieking from green parrots and someone catching their breath brought Scarlett back to the present. She pushed herself up from the ground just as Diane Harris appeared from behind some bushes.

'Bloody hell, that was steeper than I thought,' she gasped, stepping up onto the path that ringed the mound.

Scarlett turned to face her.

'Are you all right Scarlett? You look as though you're about to faint.'

Scarlett stepped to one side, giving her DCI a full view of Ella's body.

Diane slapped a hand across her mouth. 'Oh my God!'

'You can't see from there. But she'd been beheaded as well.'

'Jesus, Scarlett.'

Drawing up her face mask, Diane Harris stepped towards Ella's body. 'Come on we'll do this together. Let's see what we've got.

They stared down at Ella's corpse.

'She wasn't killed here.' Diane announced, pointing a finger. 'See, there's no blood anywhere: dried blood on the body, but nowhere else. Whoever killed Ella did it at some other place and brought her here.'

'She's been deliberately placed here like this, if you ask me.'

Diane shot Scarlett a sideways look. 'Sorry?'

'Put here, like this, on Henry the Eighth's Mound. You know the significance of this place, don't you?'

'Not with you, Scarlett?'

'This place is rumoured to be where Henry waited for the signal rocket to be fired from the Tower of London after Anne Boleyn was beheaded. This is more than a coincidence don't you think?' Scarlett couldn't tear her gaze away from Ella's severed head. The eyes were closed but her face bore a frozen look of pain, and she couldn't stop her eyes drifting down to where the metal pole protruded between her friend's legs. Scarlett shuddered. She couldn't imagine what Ella must have gone through. This was so surreal. Ella was dead. Butchered. Beheaded.

Diane Harris touched her shoulder. 'We'll get whoever did this Scarlett. Don't you worry.'

'James Green,' she said, gritting her teeth.

'You're angry.'

'Yes I fucking am. But I know it was Green. My gut tells me.'

**

Shortly after 9 a.m. Diane Harris told Scarlett she was returning to the station to brief the team, and get the murder investigation under way, leaving her to manage the scene. Scarlett didn't envy her: her boss had the daunting task of informing Ella's boyfriend, Ryan, about the discovery, though she guessed the police grapevine had already played its part in breaking the news. She was so glad she hadn't been given the job; the way she felt, she would probably have burst into tears in front of him.

Within half an hour of the DCI leaving, the Pathologist arrived. He knew the victim was the detective reported missing on the news, and he gave his heartfelt condolences to Scarlett before commencing his examination. Handling Ella's body with the utmost compassion his assessment was that she had been dead at least 12 hours and her head had been removed after death. Blood loss and shock from the assault with the metal pole were the likely cause of her death. He said his goodbye with more words of commiseration, which Scarlett thought was a wonderful gesture, and she made a note to ensure a letter of gratitude be sent to the Coroner to pass on to him. Then she waited for the forensic team. They arrived just after 10 a.m. setting up a tent over Ella's body before starting their scientific scrutiny. Scarlett liaised with the duty Inspector, and the Supervisor of the Park Police, to see how the search of the grounds had gone. Several early morning dog walkers had been stopped, but they hadn't found anyone without a legitimate excuse for being there. The park had so many access points that it was impossible to shut down the grounds and so the decision was made that only Pembroke Lodge and grounds, where Ella's body was, be sealed off. The car park outside the lodge was to be the Rendezvous Point for those coming to the scene. Diane Harris checked in with Scarlett at one o'clock, with news that they believed they had traced James Green's mother, Dorothy, to a nursing home at Feltham and they were currently firming that up. The relief almost reduced Scarlett to tears and she was about to ask if she could have the job of visiting her when the DCI ended the call. Frustrated, Scarlett returned her phone to her trouser pocket and decided she needed a coffee: no one had thought to tell the cafeteria staff not to come in, and so it was open, but because the grounds had been sealed off only officers working the crime scene could use it. In the café a couple of uniform officers were occupying a table and she acknowledged them with a brief nod as she went to the counter. She ordered a cappuccino and a toasted teacake – she suddenly realised she was hungry – and sought a table by a window, choosing to be alone: she wasn't in the mood to chat. She had just sat down when her mobile vibrated with an incoming text. It was Alex. 'Just seen it on the news about Ella. How are you.' Scarlett smiled, despite a heavy sadness overwhelming her, then texted him back, telling him she was at the scene, and that it was awful but she was dealing with it. She ended with 'Call you later.'

'Do you fancy coming to my place after work. I could cook something or get a takeaway?'

She gave his text some thought and sent, 'I don't think I will be good company.'

Seconds later came the response, 'It's always better to be miserable with someone than be miserable alone.'

That made her grin. She texted, 'I'll let you know when I finish,' and ended her message with a kiss before sending it. As she returned the phone to her pocket she felt slightly better.

Sixty-six

James Green sat in his armchair, eyes glued to the TV, watching the lunchtime news. He'd spent the morning flicking from one channel's newsreel to another, catching the breaking news about the discovery of a body in Richmond Park, where reports had gone from speculation about the victim, eventually to confirmation that it was missing Detective, Ella Bloom. For hours, his body had been tingling. With this latest news came a series of jolts that gave his head a magnificent buzz. A photograph of Ella in police uniform appeared on screen. Seeing her face fired a bolt of electricity that made him hard again. He closed his eyes. The image of Detective Bloom crying, then screaming, begging him to stop, pleading for her life, was as vivid as if she was still in front of him. He opened his eyes and returned to watching the TV. He was wired. He didn't want this unbelievable feeling to end. This was his most euphoric experience yet. It wasn't just the killing that was giving him a thrill but the getting away with it. The plan he had for Detective Macey's ending would be the icing on the cake.

Sixty-seven

In the ladies' toilets at Sutton Police Station, Scarlett stood in front of the mirror checking her make up. She added a little more mascara in an attempt to disguise her tired looking eyes. She hadn't slept a wink, even after two bottles of beer and with Alex cuddling her. All night, images of Ella's brutalised body re-ran inside her head. She hadn't been able to shake them away and now she was knackered. She thought she had learned over the years to handle death as a cop – put aside her emotion, focus on the evidence – but yesterday, all that had changed. Seeing her close colleague and friend, dumped like that, had been like a stab to the heart and stopped her functioning. She had managed to hide it, and the forensics team and uniform colleagues had done their jobs, so thanks to them the Squad had something to work with this morning. Putting away her mascara, she took a final look in the mirror, realised she was fighting a losing battle, straightened her blouse and left for the incident room.

Everyone was in. The incident board had been updated. The crime scene images of Ella were new additions, but she only gave them a glance: she did not want to be reminded again of the horror of yesterday. As she sat down she glanced at a few of her colleagues. There were no smiling faces this morning or pleasant greetings. The atmosphere was heavy. She had just placed her handbag on the floor beside her chair when her mobile rang. It was Alex. She swiped to answer. Before she had time to say anything, he said, 'Can you talk?'

She hugged the phone close to her ear and answered softly, 'Yes.'

'I've got something for you about James Green.'

His response silenced her for a couple of seconds. She responded, 'What do you mean?'

'After you showed me all those photos of his place last week, I've been doing a bit of digging around. I can't give you my sources…' He broke off, giving a half laugh. 'But when you mentioned his mother's name last night, I've got a result which I think you'll find very interesting.'

'Alex, that's great.'

'Have you got a pen and paper handy?'

Clamping the phone between ear and shoulder, she rummaged around her desk, snatching up a pen and several sheets of scrap paper. 'Pen poised with bated breath,' she said.

Alex laughed. 'And you can't say where this came from. You did your own digging around, okay?'

'That's good with me. It means I'll get all the brownie points.'

'Okay, you were right to think that James Green might not be his real name. I don't think it is. I've been able to access Dorothy Green's data, and she did have a son called James, but he died in 2004, aged seven. I can't get much else without questions being asked, but it's a good start for you. Dorothy should be able to fill in the dots. Didn't you say she was in a care home?'

'Nursing home, somewhere in Feltham. I think it's one of the tasks this morning to visit her.'

'Well it'll give you something to talk to her about, but it's left you with the mystery of not knowing who your guy really is.'

'I know, but that's a real help and it's reinforced my thoughts about him.'

'Listen, I might be able to help you a little further.'

'What with?'

'Didn't you say that Ella had received a call on her BlackBerry purporting to be from the communications room?'

'Yes. We've accessed her phone records. It's a mobile number. It's with the technicians. They're still working on it.'

'Look, give me the number and I'll use the resources I've got. He'll have left a footprint which might help pinpoint where he is. I should be able to get something in a couple of hours.'

'You sure?'

'Sure. And ask no questions Scarlett. This didn't come from me.'

'One day I'm going to find out what you do, Alex King, although I think I already know.'

'Remember what I said, if I tell you, I'll have to kill you.'

It was her turn to laugh.

'Now give me the mobile number.'

She had just passed Alex the mobile number from Ella's BlackBerry and ended her call, when Lucy walked into the office holding aloft a padded envelope. 'The receptionist downstairs asked me to give you this. It was left at the counter.'

Scarlett took the padded envelope from her, turned it over and recognised the handwriting.

Sixty-eight

Scarlett dropped the package as if it was a hot potato and stared at the writing. James Green's name exploded inside her head, even though she now knew this was more than likely a false one. Everyone crowded over her and she glanced up. Diane Harris and Hayden Taylor-Butler had joined the group.

She said, 'It's the same writing as on his bedroom wall and on the other packages I've been sent.' She reached inside her desk drawer, took out a pair of latex gloves and pulled them on. With finger and thumb, she picked up the padded envelope by a corner, and angling it, slowly slid out its contents. It was a DVD in its case. Most of her colleagues looked puzzled. She took out the DVD and inserted it into her computer. The room was silent as the whirring disc loaded up. After a few seconds the screen flashed and then a picture emerged. It was Ella. A full body shot of her, fastened to a chair. Someone behind Scarlett gasped. The camera zoomed in to capture an upper body shot. Scarlett could see dried and congealed blood on the left-hand side of her friend's head. Ella was crying, soft moans drifting through the tape across her mouth. Her nose was snotting and she was struggling to breathe. Scarlett's stomach lurched. Bile rose in her throat and she swallowed hard. A burning sensation to the back of her throat caused her to blink. She was about to heave again and put a hand to her mouth in a vain attempt at stopping herself from being sick. She knew it wasn't going to work and grabbed the waste basket. She threw up as she got the metal basket to chest height. Her vomit hit the edge. Her second wave of vomit slapped the bottom.

In the ladies, Lucy patted Scarlett's shoulder as she splashed water over her face and scooped cold water from the tap to rinse out her mouth.

'Are you okay?'

Scarlett gripped the edge of the sink and looked in the mirror. She was pale. 'Sorry Lucy I couldn't stop myself.'

Lucy gently massaged the back of Scarlett's neck. 'Don't apologise. None of us expected that. We've got to catch this bastard.'

Scarlett could see the colour beginning to return to her face. She let go of the sink and straightened, taking in a deep breath. She let it out slowly.

'Feeling better?' Lucy asked.

'A lot better, thank you.' Scarlett grabbed a handful of paper towels and wiped her face and mouth. The strength in her legs had returned. Screwing up the towels and binning them, she faced Lucy and said, 'Come on let's go and see if we can find James Green. We can't let him get away with this.'

They headed back to the incident room. As Scarlett drew level with the gents she heard muffled curses coming from inside. It sounded like Taylor-Butler. A sudden flashback jogged her memory. Her first wave of vomit had sprayed over the edge of the waste paper basket and the DI's trousers had been showered. As she passed the toilet door, she turned and looked at Lucy. They burst into a fit of laughter.

Sixty-nine

Scarlett was at the office door with Lucy when her mobile went. It was Alex, so she told Lucy to go ahead, and retreated onto the back stairs, stepping down to the ground floor while answering.

'Hi Alex.'

'Can you talk?'

'Yes, no one can hear.'

'I promised I'd get back to you about the number you needed tracing.'

'Crikey Alex, that was quick.'

'I have some good contacts. I'm guessing your tech team haven't come back to you yet.'

'Not as far as I'm aware. Morning briefing has been delayed.' She told him about the DVD and how it had affected her.

'Good God Scarlett, are you okay?'

'I am now thanks.'

'I'd hate to be this guy when you catch up with him. And on that note, I've got something that might help you.'

'Brilliant.'

'The number is a pay and go, just as I expected and he hasn't used it for long before taking it off line. It was first activated at 14.22 hours the day before Ella was abducted. My guess is that he was testing the SIM card and that's where he's slipped up. That activation was in a building on Lemon Grove at Feltham, but the phone was only on for just over a minute before it was switched off again. The beauty about modern phones is that they give GPS locations, and I've Google Mapped the location to a block of high rise flats called Belvedere Place. The check doesn't pinpoint the exact address, so you're going to have to do some work on that.'

'Alex that's really great, thank you.'

'The next activation is 00.03 hrs when the call was made to Ella's BlackBerry. That call was made from Deptford. He was on the A202 and I've been able to follow the signal all the way to the industrial site at Greenwich, where Ella was abducted, so it looks as though he was in a vehicle. The signal went off at the industrial estate at 00.28, and it hasn't been activated since, so I'm guessing he's removed and destroyed the SIM card. Or at least he will have done if he's any sense. I'm going to text you the GPS locations and the times so you can check your roadside cameras.'

'Alex that's fantastic.'

'Your tech unit should be able to give you the same, but it's given you the heads up to start doing some digging.'

'I owe you one Alex.'

'More than one, I think. You and I have a date the moment you finish this case. A proper date!'

'Deal,' she answered breaking into a grin. 'And now Alex King, some of us have work to do. Can't stand chatting to you all day.' Before he could respond she finished the call.

She took the stairs back to the incident room two at a time. At the top she just avoided colliding with Hayden Taylor-Butler. He had a face like thunder and she made her smirk vanish.

She said, 'Sorry boss, didn't see you there. I'm just going into briefing.'

The DI stopped in front of the doors, blocking her way and glowered at her.

Scarlett couldn't miss the damp patches down the front of his trousers. It looked like he had pissed himself and she wanted to laugh, but she daren't. Holding in her stomach she brushed past him, pushing open the doors. 'Sorry about the accident,' she said.

Diane Harris was taking morning briefing. The DCI broke off, ushered her and the DI in and continued. The DCI was allocating tasks. As Scarlett took her seat, Diane Harris said, 'Scarlett, I was just telling George, I want you and him to carry on working together until Tarn returns. We have finally traced Dorothy Green to a nursing home near Grosvenor Park at

Feltham. I want you two to go and see if she is related to our James Green, and if she is, get some background history and an address for him.'

Scarlett hadn't shared the information Alex had given her about James Green being Dorothy's dead son. She had been wondering how to feed it in and a perfect opportunity had been handed to her. She acknowledged the DCI's request with a nod.

Seventy

The nursing home where Dorothy Green was being cared for was a two-storey modern complex in its own grounds, just a street away from Grosvenor Park. Scarlett found a parking spot and she and George walked across the car park to an entrance, with automatic double doors. The reception area was large and well lit, the walls adorned with colourful framed prints. Two young women in lilac scrubs were chatting behind a light oak counter-cum-work-station. They fell silent as Scarlett and George approached. Scarlett showed her warrant card and explained the purpose of their visit.

'I'm one of the carers here. You do know that Dorothy has early onset dementia don't you?' The woman was in her early twenties with flaxen coloured hair, tied high in a ponytail. Her English accent was tinged with Eastern European.

'We want to ask her about her son.' Scarlett responded. 'Is she able to talk to us? Would she be able to answer questions about him?'

'Dorothy has good days and bad. Which son do you want to talk to her about?'

Scarlett glanced at George, then turned her attention to the carer. 'She has more than one son?'

The young woman's drawn-on eyebrows knitted together. 'Oh yes. Well she had. One of them is dead though. I believe he died in a house fire a few years ago. She constantly goes on about him.'

'His name wouldn't be James by any chance, would it?'

The young woman nodded. 'Yes, that's him. I think he was only young when he died. That's the impression I get when she talks about him. I believe she lost her husband in the same fire. I don't know any details, it's just what Dorothy has mentioned when she has her good days.'

'And this other son?' Scarlett asked.

The carer looked to the receptionist, a woman in her mid-to-late thirties.

'Do you recall the name of the man who visits Dorothy?' The carer asked.

'I can check through the signing-in book,' said the receptionist. She lifted a heavy bound volume off the counter and began to flip back the pages.

'The man comes regularly to see Dorothy?' Scarlett asked.

'Fairly regularly. Twice a week at least,' said the carer.

Scarlett reached into her bag and pulled out the mug shot of James Green, holding it out for them to see. 'Is this the man who visits her?'

The carer nodded, 'Yes that's him.'

'Jason Cabett!' the receptionist responded, looking up from the signing-in book. She had her finger over an entry. 'He was here three days ago to see his mum. He always brings her flowers. Nice young man. Always polite. Sometimes brings chocolates for us.'

Scarlett asked, 'You don't have an address by any chance?'

***

Walking across the car park to their vehicle, Scarlett rang Diane Harris and relayed to her what they had just been told. The DCI ordered them back to the station and called an early briefing.

'We didn't need to see Dorothy after all,' Scarlett addressed her colleagues. 'The nursing home provided us with enough info to enable us to do some digging without talking to her. When we got back, I put in a call to the *Feltham Chronicle's* archive section, gave them what we'd got about the death of James Green in a house fire and asked them to do some searches for us. It took a good hour, but they came back with everything I needed.' Scarlett scoured the room, a thin smile on her face. She was doing her best to hide her smug feeling. 'There's two important parts to this. The first, which is very relevant, relates to her first marriage. That was to a man called Thomas Cabett, in 1988. Thomas Cabett is a very interesting man and I'll come on to him in a bit.' She took a short breath. 'Two years after they were married, in 1990, they had a son, Jason. When we showed the care staff the photo we have of James Green, they told us they knew him as Dorothy's son Jason.' She saw a number of her colleagues faces light up. 'They say he is a regular visitor there. Always brings his mum flowers. And the flowers bit fits in with what we learned from James Green's neighbour at Twickenham.' She stopped for a moment, then said, 'Is everyone following me?' Several of the team nodded. 'Now I'll go back to Jason's father, Thomas. The paper has quite a bit of information about him.' Scarlett glanced down at her notes. 'I said to you that Thomas is a very interesting man. Well, Thomas had a teenage history of arson, which resulted in him being sent to a young offender's institution. Apparently in 1980, at the age of fourteen, he set fire to a number of cars in Feltham, for which he received an eighteen-month sentence. He came out when he was fifteen and a couple of years later he met Dorothy. They married when he was twenty-two. At some stage, in between that, he became a carpenter. Jason was born when Thomas was twenty-four. Five years later, in 1995, Thomas set fire to a pub in Feltham, and one of the bar staff, who rented the flat above the pub, was killed. Although convicted of manslaughter, Thomas was assessed to be mentally unfit and detained in a medium secure mental health unit. He is still there. I got all of this background, and the background to the fire, from the articles they wrote about him during his trial. According to those stories, he had been working at the pub, doing a refit of the bar, but had fallen out with the company who owned the pub, over payment. In a drunken rage one night he'd set fire to the pub, not realising someone was living in the flat above.' She explored the faces of the squad again. She had their attention, 'And now I come on to James Green. In 1997, Dorothy marries a man called David Green.' Pausing, she broke away from the main flow of her story, 'I got that from the hatched, matched and dispatched section of the *Chronicle*. I'm surmising she divorced Thomas while he was in the secure unit.' Picking up the thread again, she said, 'That same year, six months after her marriage, James was born.' She looked around the room again. 'And this is where it gets really interesting. In 2004, there was a fire at the house where they all lived, on Waterloo Close, at Feltham. David and James died. Jason, who was fourteen at the time, apparently rescued his mother. There was quite a big article in the *Chronicle* about it. He was praised as a hero. The fire was recorded as an accident; David was a smoker and it was reported the fire had started in the chair where David normally sat. David and James are buried in Feltham Cemetery. James was only seven. Jason and his mother were re-housed in a flat at Belvedere House, in Feltham.'

Diane Harris interrupted, 'So, let me get this right Scarlett, what you are saying is that Jason Cabett, Dorothy's first son, has taken the identity of James Green, her second son, who was killed in a house fire.'

Scarlett nodded. 'That's what I believe.' After holding the DCI's gaze for a few seconds, she said, 'And do you want the piece de resistance?'

'There's more?' Diane Harris responded.

Scarlett smiled broadly. 'Oh, there's more all right. Although he never gives his address when he signs in at the care home, on a hunch, I rang the housing department and gave them Dorothy's name and asked them to do a check at Belvedere House at Feltham. And guess what?' Before anyone had time to answer Scarlett said, 'The rent of the flat at Belvedere House, in Dorothy's name, is still being paid.' She exhaled sharply. She didn't need to tell them about Alex's trace of the number that had appeared on Ella's phone, which located back to Belvedere House. She had crossed the T's and dotted the I's with her own phone calls.

Ella's killer was in touching distance.

Seventy-one

The next morning, a three-vehicle convoy made its way to Belvedere House. The first two vehicles – marked vans – contained officers from the Task Force, suited and booted, ready for the raid of Dorothy's flat. Scarlett and George, with Detectives Carl Jenkins and Kathryn Hall, from Syndicate Two, followed up the rear in an unmarked car. Belvedere House was just behind Feltham shopping centre, part of a twin concrete complex of high rise flats. Dorothy's flat was on the fourth floor. Apartment 416.

The police fleet pulled up on a side road, kitted up – the Task Force adding body armour to their overalls, and the Homicide Squad donning forensic suits – and then they made their way to the main entrance at a trot. Two officers stayed in the foyer, guarding the lifts, just in case their target was already making his way down and the rest of the team took the stairs. At the top of the stairwell of the fourth floor, everyone grabbed a breath and composed themselves. Then, following a silent signal from the Task Force Sergeant, they hurried along the balcony to apartment 416. It took two swings with the steel enforcer to smash in the door and then everyone rushed inside. All the rooms were on one floor, and Scarlett and her team stayed by the broken door, listening as officers cleared each room.

When the last shout went up Scarlett was disappointed. Jason Cabett, aka James Green, wasn't here. Flashing her team a frustrated look, she flicked her head and ordered, 'Come on let's start searching the place.'

She was about to take the first door to her left when a voice shouted from up ahead and one of the Task Force officers stepped into the doorway at the far end of the hallway. 'You need to take a look in here,' he said. Scarlett caught sight of a single bed pushed against the wall. The room behind him was bathed in a diffused orange light indicating that the curtains were closed. She stopped at the doorway and looked inside. The coruscating light coming through the cheap orange curtains cast everything in a warm glow. But there was nothing warm or cosy about the interior. The bedroom was drab and poorly furnished, the furniture years out of date. Beside the single bed, in the three-metre by three-metre room, there was a single wardrobe in a corner to her left and a set of drawers. What caught her eye was the chair on the plastic sheeting in the centre of the room, a large orange/brown stain surrounding it. She recognised this scene from the DVD she had been sent. *This is where Ella had been killed.* Her head felt as if it was exploding; a rush of meteorites whizzed behind her eyes and she went light-headed. Feeling her legs about to give way she grabbed for the door handle and sucked in a series of deep breaths. Within a few seconds the fainting sensation receded and the strength returned to her legs. As the flashes subsided and her vision returned she took in the room again. Next to the set of drawers was a small video camera on a tripod that she had missed from her initial sweep. And then, her gaze fastened on the montage of photographs taped to the wall: photographs of her and of Ella.

***

Driving his mother's car, Jason Cabett turned off Feltham High Street, heading back to his flat. He had got up early to begin clearing the place of incriminating evidence. The day before he had smashed Detective Ella Bloom's phone to smithereens and, together with the SIM card from his own phone, had tossed them into nearby Queen Mary Reservoir. That morning he had bin-bagged the detective's clothing and his own blood-stained T-shirt and joggers, and driven over to a refuse site at Hounslow and dumped them into a skip. It had been out of his way, and had taken him over an hour, because of the traffic, but the journey had been worth it. No one would think of looking there. All he had left to do was to get rid of the chair and the plastic sheeting: he had already identified another dump-it site, five miles away, at Staines. As he approached Lemon Grove, where Belvedere House was located, he was feeling rather chuffed with himself; another two hours' work and there would be nothing the cops could pin on him, even if they did track him down. He was so caught up in his thoughts that he almost missed the riot vans tucked against the side of the flats. He braked sharply. A car horn blared and he shot a glance in his rear-view mirror: he hadn't thought about who had been behind him, so swift had been his panic reaction. A silver VW Polo swung out and overtook with a screech of tyres, the young male driver giving him a tosser handshake as he passed. He caught his breath and a knot formed in his stomach as he looked at the leading police van parked in the road opposite. He also spotted the white Vauxhall Astra, third in line, recognising it as one of the cars he had seen Detective Macey in. *She'd found him. Fuck. She'll have found the evidence as well.* Detective Macey had fucked up all his plans. He was screwed. His heart started thumping and he could hear rushing noises in his ears. He drew in a deep breath. He needed to regain control. He still had something to finish. Putting the car in first gear, he turned slowly left, out from the junction – leaving behind his hiding place for the past eighteen months – and headed out of town, towards Richmond, where he could formulate new plans.

***

'It looks as if he's been following me and Ella around ever since he was released from court. I recognise where he's taken most of the photographs we found in the bedroom, from their background.' Scarlett turned towards DI Taylor-Butler in the squad room, fixed him with a stare, and added, 'I told you he's been stalking me.' Satisfied she'd stabbed her point home, she returned to updating everyone about the investigation. It was now 8 p.m. Scarlett and her team had been at Dorothy Green's flat most of the day, searching through everything to see if they could get a location for Jason Cabett. From speaking with neighbours, they knew he had been staying there ever since the collapse of his rape trial, and from the warm kettle and half empty mug of coffee they had found in the kitchen, they had only just missed him. In a drawer in the lounge sideboard, they had found the registration document for his mother's blue Ford Fiesta and had run it through the Police National Computer. Some of the team had gone back through footage from roadside cameras on the night Ella had been abducted, and had picked out the car at various points leading to the industrial site at Greenwich. The next job was to look through today's camera recordings to find where the Fiesta was now. At the flat, a forensic team, including photographers and an exhibits officer had been brought in and they had made a start on evidence gathering. A lot of ground had been covered since they had found the place where Ella had been butchered.

Diane Harris thanked Scarlett and took over. 'I know everyone is psyched up but there's nothing much else we can do today folks. Jason Cabett has been circulated, as has his mother's vehicle. It is only a matter of time before we catch him. I want everyone's fresh eye on this, and I can see you're flagging so I'm going to call it a day. I want everyone back in for 7a.m. tomorrow.' Solemnly, the DCI ran her gaze around the room. 'Good work everyone, and before you go, let me remind you all it's Trish Scarr's funeral tomorrow. I know some of you will want to pay your respects and support Tarn.'

Seventy-two

St. John The Evangelist, Roman Catholic Church, was at the edge of a housing estate, overshadowed by a huge concrete rail flyover. It was the church where Tarn Scarr had married Trish five years earlier and now it was where he would say his final farewell to her.

Scarlett, George Martin and another close team member, Phil Foster, stood uneasily by the gate, watching the funeral cortege slowly approach. It hadn't come far – Trish's parents lived two streets away. The coffin bearer car rolled past them and drew up a few yards away. Through the windows Scarlett saw the word MUMMY, spelled out in individual letters with pink carnations, resting against the side of the coffin and her stomach flipped. The lead passenger car stopped directly in front of them, capturing her attention. A funeral attendant jumped out and opened the back doors and she got her first glimpse of Tarn in over a week. Looking sad and drawn, he was a shadow of himself, and she wondered how he was going to cope, especially with two such young children. Would he return to work? She met Tarn's eyes as he exited the car. He looked grief-stricken and acknowledged her with the ghost of a smile. Her chest lurched as she suppressed a sob. He helped his children, Dale and Heather, out of the car, their faces a picture of confusion as they looked among the throng of mourners. It was as if they didn't know what was happening. *Maybe they didn't. That probably wasn't a bad thing.* Tarn's parents climbed out after him, and following an exchange of sad glances with their son, they tearfully hugged one another and moved to the coffin bearing vehicle.

The third black vehicle in the cortege contained Trish's parents and a woman, who looked to be early thirties. Scarlett couldn't help but notice how like Trish she was. A sister? Scarlett didn't know Trish had a sister. She watched her file past with her parents. The resemblance to Trish was uncanny. She could almost be her twin. She watched them join Tarn, Dale and Heather, and his parents and exchange sombre nods.

Then everyone waited and watched as Trish's light oak coffin was pulled from the back of the car by the team of bearers, hoisted up onto their shoulders, and with such well-practised grace, shuffled sideways to face the entrance of the church. With a final check from the funeral director, the march into church began.

Scarlett and her colleagues waited until last. As they entered, Gary Barlow's *Let Me Go* was playing, and, although an upbeat tune, Scarlett knew the significance of the song and she felt her chest lurch again. Taking a pew, she picked up the order of service leaflet, glanced at it fleetingly and drew in a deep breath. She wasn't looking forward to this. If truth be told she didn't want to be here. She would rather have been back at the station working on capturing Jason Cabett, but Tarn was her closest colleague on the squad and her friend and if roles were switched she knew he'd be doing exactly the same for her. In a week or two's time she would be going through this again at Ella's funeral and she knew she wouldn't hold it together then. As the song faded she took in another deep breath.

It was her first time at a Catholic funeral service and it seemed awfully long, prolonging the agony. Scarlett drifted in and out; if she paid too much attention to the words being said she would end up bursting into tears and making a spectacle of herself. She was glad when it finally ended and she could leave.

Outside, she caught another glimpse of Tarn. His eyes were red but his attention rested on his children and Scarlett thought that was a good thing. There would be many times over the next few weeks when he would feel alone and grieve but having Dale and Heather around would ensure it wasn't all the time. She watched him guide them back into the funeral car, joining his parents; they were going on to the cemetery for the burial: Scarlett was going to avoid that – work was pressing and they had a killer to catch.

***

Back at the station, Scarlett made herself a coffee and took two paracetamols; she could feel a headache coming on and didn't want it to stop her over the remainder of the day. She found Lucy Summers and caught up with what was happening. Jason's mother's car had been identified and tracked from the previous day's roadside camera footage – they had only missed him by whisker when they had raided the flat. A team were out, currently going over the ground where the car had been spotted, seeing if there was anything relevant about the journey he had made earlier the previous day. Jason had returned while they were searching the flat, obviously spotted them and taken avoiding action. They had managed to track the car for another few miles, as it had diverted away to Staines along the A308, but then it disappeared. The theory was it had either been dumped in an estate somewhere or Jason had switched number plates. Lucy finished by telling her that the DCI was currently with a news broadcasting team recording an appeal for the local evening news – tonight, the public of London were going to get their first view of the face of a cop-killer.

Scarlett thanked Lucy for the update and was about to check what tasks had been allocated to her when her desk phone went. It was one of the receptionists from downstairs.

She said, 'Scarlett, another of those packages has just been handed in. It was an old man. I've got his details. He said it was given to him ten minutes ago by a youngish guy wearing a hoodie. He gave him a tenner to bring it in for him.'

'Okay I'll be down in a couple of ticks.'

Pulling on a pair of latex gloves, Scarlett headed to reception, recovered the padded envelope and returned to her desk. Like the others it was addressed to Detective Macey and written in the same hand. Taking her time, she gently peeled open the seal and tipped out its contents, wondering what it would be this time. A candle fell from the package, rolling until a small pile of papers brought it to a halt. She shook her head. This just didn't make sense. Whatever game Jason Cabett was playing, she wasn't on his wavelength. She returned her attention to the package, looking inside. There was a small piece of paper. Tipping the envelope upside down she shook it. The slip of paper fell out.

Penned, boldly in ink, were the words, HERE COMES THE CANDLE.

Seventy-three

Scarlett turned the key in the lock and pushed her front door open as she let out a heavy sigh. It had been a long day. A long couple of days. She was whacked. All she wanted was to grab a quick bite, soak in the bath and flop into her comfy bed. Dragging herself out of her biking leathers, she went through to the kitchen, checked what she had by the way of food in the fridge, made a cheese and salad sandwich, grabbed a yoghurt, and suddenly feeling less drained, decided to hold off on the soak in the bath and grab an hour's TV to unwind. Besides, she wanted to see the DCI's appeal on the news. No matter how tired she felt, she wouldn't be able to relax enough to drop off immediately unless she unwound a little. Taking her sandwich and yoghurt through to the lounge she dropped onto the sofa, switched on her TV with the remote and settled back into the cushions. There was just under an hour before the news, so she whizzed through the TV planner, channel-hopped a couple of programmes and settled on the final part of *24 hours in A & E*; it was easy viewing that she didn't have to concentrate on, and she also liked to draw comparisons with the other emergency services who coped with limited resources.

Finishing her sandwich and yoghurt she drew her legs up beneath her, took in the remainder of the hospital programme and as it ended switched channels. The piece about Jason Cabett featured on the local London news. It showed footage of the abandoned industrial site where Ella had been abducted, the garden at Pembroke Lodge in Richmond Park, close to where her body had been found and finished with a shot of Jason's Mother's flat at Belvedere House. The photograph they showed of him was the mugshot taken following his arrest for rape, four months earlier, when he was known as James Green. The news production team had given it a good airing. As she switched off the TV she hoped that by the morning someone would have rung in and grassed him up for the £5,000 reward they were offering.

After tidying up the kitchen, she wearily climbed the stairs, undressed, bathed, put on her nightwear and climbed into her inviting double bed. The events of the past few days had finally caught up with her. As she plumped up her pillow she could feel her brain starting to shut down even before she rested her head. Turning off the bedside light, she pulled the duvet up to her chin and closed her eyes.

***

Jason Cabett stepped out of the shadows opposite Scarlett's home. Her house was now in darkness. For the past hour he'd been watching her shadow drift past curtained windows. He could tell by the flashes through the curtains that she had watched some TV when she got home. The last thing he'd seen before the house had been plunged into darkness was her bathroom light being turned off. The front bedroom light hadn't gone on and he guessed she slept in the back. He picked up his bag and hugged it close to his chest. He would give it another half hour, then he would put the final part of his plan into action.

***

A loud beeping noise woke Scarlett and for a split second she was bewildered. It was not only pitch black but something cloudy was snaking across her vision. Suddenly her chest was tight and she couldn't breathe. The back of her throat stung. She started to cough, her chest getting even tighter. She tried to gasp in air. Panicking, she flung out a hand, searching for the bedside light. She switched it on, still trying to catch her breath. As the room lit up she saw why. The bedroom was full of smoke. Thick, dark smoke! Her house was on fire! Flinging aside her duvet, she launched herself out of bed. Her chest was so tight now it burned. She was going to die if she didn't get out of here. The smoke was coming from the landing, or downstairs. She couldn't see any flames though. The shrill beeping noise of the smoke alarm resounded from the hallway. Stumbling, she slammed the bedroom door shut and tried to take in a gulp of air. The smoke hit the back of her throat and another wracking coughing fit started, causing her to stumble. Only the closed door stopped her from hitting the floor. She had to get out. Struggling back to her bed, she rolled across it to the window and almost ripped the curtains off the pole as she flung them aside. Then she threw open the side window, flinging her head outside. She grabbed for air, desperate to breathe, but her throat was clogged and another bout of coughing started, tightening her chest even further. The patio was below her. She checked where the potted plants and her garden bench were. This was her only way out. Exerting everything she had left, she grabbed hold of the window frame and pulled herself up onto the sill. Then, swinging out her legs she hauled herself over the sill, dropping the fifteen feet or so to the ground. She hit the paved patio feet first, hearing a loud crack and feeling her right ankle turn under her. The pain was excruciating, adding to the soreness in her chest, and a blaze of fireworks exploded inside her head. She fell forward, letting out a yelp, throwing out her hands to stop her head hitting the ground. Closing her eyes, she forced herself to breathe. Every part of her body screamed with pain. Then she heard a voice, a melodious, singing sound. She opened her eyes to see where it was coming from. It sounded close to the fence surrounding her small garden, only a couple of yards away. She could just make out some form of human shape in the dark. Her brain was trying to make out what the song was. She had heard it before: something from her past. The shape stepped nearer and the singing became louder. The voice was mocking. And, in that instant she both recognised the voice and the song. It was Jason Cabett, and he was chanting a nursery rhyme that her Grandfather Macey used to sing – *Oranges and Lemons*. Images burst into her thoughts: the items she had been sent, the messages written by Jason Cabett, were all in that rhyme. It was all coming together. She saw the dark spectre edging towards her, the silhouette beginning to take on form, the head lowering.

'Here comes the candle, to light you to bed,' Jason shrieked as he came ever closer.

Scarlett knew what the next line was – and the glint of something shiny flashed at the end of his arm.

A knife!

Still struggling for breath, she made a last scrambled effort to push herself up. Her right hand nudged something and she closed her fingers around it. A pebble: one of the large pebbles she and her aunt had brought back from Brighton beach to decorate the garden. It was as big as her hand. She grabbed it.

'And here comes a chopper to chop off your head.' Jason laughed. He sounded maniacal.

As he bent towards her, in one desperate effort Scarlett lunged, arcing her hand to where she thought Jason's head would be. She felt the pebble strike home, and there was a sharp crack followed by a loud yell. The momentum flung her forward, onto him and they fell sideways together. She brought down the rock again and then everything faded to black.

Seventy-four

A gentle beeping noise drifted into her thoughts. A cold draught tickled the back of her throat. Then, the tightness in her chest gripped again and she began to panic. A bright light sparked inside her head the moment she flung open her eyes. Where was she?

A hand wrapped around hers, giving it a squeeze and a voice said, 'Hey, careful. You're okay. You're safe.' As the flares subsided Alex's concerned face came into view. He was unshaven and his dark hair a tousled mess. *Still looks damn sexy though*. As her vision widened she realised she was in hospital. The gentle beeping was her heart monitor and the cold draught came from the oxygen tubes up her nose.

'What happened?' A flicker of images entered her thoughts. 'Jason Cabett.'

Alex squeezed her hand tighter and leaned in. 'You got him.'

Her brain started piecing together what had happened. Slowly the visions began filing themselves in order. 'I got him?'

Alex nodded.

'He was going to kill me.'

'We know, but you got him.'

She remembered grabbing the large pebble, targeting it at his head. 'Did I hit him?'

Alex gave a hearty laugh. 'Hit him is an understatement.'

'What?'

'You almost caved his skull in.'

'What?' Scarlett tried to push herself up, setting off a fit of coughing which brought back the pains to her chest.

Alex gently pushed her back against the supporting pillows. 'Careful, Scarlett. The smoke from the fire has damaged your lungs and throat. You've also got a badly sprained ankle. You shouldn't be exerting yourself.'

'Jason set my house on fire?' It was a rhetorical question.

Alex nodded.

'Is there much damage?'

'Nothing that the insurance can't fix.'

'What about Jason?'

'He's just down the corridor. He's in a side ward. There's a police guard on him, and your DCI, Diane Harris, is in there with him, but he's not going anywhere for a long time.'

'Did I hurt him much? You said I almost caved his skull in. Was that a joke?'

'You gave him a hell of a whack Scarlett. You've fractured his skull in two places. He's got a bleed to the brain. They've put him in an induced coma.'

'Is he going to die?'

Alex shrugged his shoulders. 'I wouldn't think so, but he's going to have a hell of a sore head when he wakes up.' He let out another laugh. 'He got what he deserved. Your DCI told me they found a machete.'

'How did they find me?'

'A bit of luck apparently. One of your patrols came across his mother's car in the next street to yours and then they saw the front of your house on fire. The officers climbed over your back fence and found you both unconscious.'

'Jesus.'

Alex shook his head and smiled.

'You certainly lead a very exciting life, Scarlett Macey.'

She started to laugh and set off the coughing again. Whacking her chest, she squirmed. 'Ouch, that hurts.'

Alex massaged her shoulder, 'Look, you need to take it easy Scarlett.'

'How long have I got to stay in here?'

He threw her a 'don't know' look, and said, 'A couple of days?'

'A couple of days!'

'What's a couple of days? I know one thing Scarlett Macey, when you do get out, you and I are going for that meal you promised. And it's all on you for scaring me like this.'

'Is that you actually saying you care?'

He smiled. 'I wouldn't push it that far.'

They burst into laughter together, causing a fresh bout of coughing.

Oranges and Lemons
Oranges and Lemons,
Say the bells of St. Clement's.
You owe me five farthings,
Say the bells of St Martin's.
When will you pay me?
Say the bells of Old Bailey.
When I grow rich,
Say the bells of Shoreditch.
When will that be?
Say the bells of Stepney.
I do not know,
Say the great bells of Bow.
Here comes the candle to light you to bed,
And here comes a chopper to chop off your head.
(Chip chop, chip chop, the last man's dead).

Oranges and Lemons was the name of a square-four-eight-dance published in 1665, but it is not clear if the dance relates to this rhyme. It is however popular as an old nursery rhyme, the words also used in a child's singing game of the same name.

Various theories have been put forward to account for the words in the rhyme, including: that it deals with child sacrifices; that it describes executions; that it describes Henry VIII's marital difficulties.

The earliest recorded version of the rhyme appeared in a song book in 1744.

Today, the bells of St. Clement Danes ring out the tune of the rhyme.

Acknowledgements

The settings for some of this story came from a great weekend visit to Richmond-upon-Thames courtesy of my good friend Giles Brearley.

I would like to thank Claire Knight for generously reading the original manuscript and critiquing its content. She has given me a great idea for the next Scarlett Macey book – thank you.

I am so grateful to my editor Sandra Mangan for making a 'silk purse out of a sow's ear'.

To my wife Liz, and to my granddaughter Scarlett, for reminding me that there is something else that is just as much fun as writing.

To Darren Laws at Caffeine Nights Publishing, who works tirelessly to support and promote my work.

And finally, thank you to all those readers who keep sending me kind messages and reviews and invite me to talk at their groups – I couldn't be without you.